D1617463

EVELYN SCOTT (1893–1963) was born in Clarksville,
Tennessee, and moved to New Orleans in her early teens.
At twenty, she caused a scandal among the Louisiana aris-
tocracy by eloping with a man twenty-four years her sen-
ior—Cyril Kay Scott—adopting a pseudonym (she was
born Elsie Dunn), and moving to a Brazilian plantation.
The hardships of life in South America, hardships to which
she was not accustomed, caused Evelyn to begin looking
homeward, and she launched upon her long writing career
by submitting work to American literary magazines, among
them *Poetry* and *The Egoist*. She soon earned in intellectual
circles the reputation of a literary enigma.

On returning to the United States in 1919, Evelyn became
immersed in the artistic and sexual progressiveness of bohe-
mian Greenwich Village. Her radicalism extended to almost every strand of American intellectual life in the
interwar years: from feminism to Freud, from anarchism to
the art colonies of Taos and Santa Fe. She championed the
writing of James Joyce, Jean Rhys, and William Faulkner.
A prolific artist, in the period between 1921 and 1941 she
wrote twelve novels, two volumes of poetry, four children's
books, and two autobiographical works. Her novels earned
her great critical acclaim, particularly *The Narrow House*
(1921), *Migrations* (1927), and *The Wave* (1929).

THE
NARROW HOUSE

BY
EVELYN SCOTT

SHORELINE BOOKS

an imprint of
W · W · NORTON & COMPANY · NEW YORK · LONDON

Library of Congress Cataloging-in-Publication Data

Scott, Evelyn, 1893–1963
The narrow house.

I. Title.
PS3537.C89N37   1986   813'52   86–121

ISBN 0-87140-142-8

W. W. Norton & Company, Inc., 500 Fifth Avenue, New York, N. Y. 10110
W. W. Norton & Company Ltd., 37 Great Russell Street, London WC1B 3NU

1   2   3   4   5   6   7   8   9   0

"*Love seeketh only Self to please,*
To bind another to its delight,
Joys in another's loss of ease,
And builds a hell in heaven's despite."

—WILLIAM BLAKE

THE NARROW HOUSE

THE NARROW HOUSE

PART I

THE hot, bright street looked almost deserted. A sign swung before the disheveled building at the corner and on a purple ground one could read the notice, "Robinson & Son, Builders," painted in tall white letters. Some broken plaster had been thrown from one of the windows and lay on the dusty sidewalk in a glaring heap.

The old-fashioned house next door was as badly in need of improvements as the one undergoing alterations. The dingy brick walls were streaked by the drippage from the leaky tin gutter that ran along the roof. The massive shutters, thrown back from the long windows, were rotting away. Below the lifted panes very clean worn curtains hung slack like things exhausted by the heat.

Some papers had been thrust in the tin letter box before the clumsy dark green door, and as Mrs. Farley emerged from the house she stopped to glance at them before descending to the street. One of the papers had a Kansas City postmark and she thought it must have come for her husband from a certain woman whom she was trying to forget. She placed the papers clumsily back where she had found them.

As she passed down the stone stairs she stooped to toss a bright scrap of orange peel to the gutter. She sighed as she did it, not even taking the trouble to brush the dust from the shabby white cotton gloves she wore. Her skirt was too long behind and as she dragged her feet across the pavement it swept the ground after her. She glanced into the place which was being repaired and wished that something might be done to improve her home. At any rate now that her daughter-in-law, Winnie, had become reconciled to her parents things would be better. Mr. and Mrs. Price were rich. They had a carriage and an automobile. Mrs. Farley told herself that it was because of her grandchildren that the end of the long family quarrel brought some relief. Winnie's two babies, a girl and a boy, would now enjoy many things which the Farleys had not been able to provide. Mrs. Farley thought of them going to church in Mrs. Price's fine carriage. Mrs. Farley knew that she should have taken the part of her son, Laurence, who had been responsible for the disagreement, but somehow it had been impossible to condemn Winnie. The poor girl was not strong. Laurie was a harsh man. He was stubborn. He did not forgive easily and would suffer everything rather than admit himself in the wrong. He had been like that as a youth. And idly, as one in a boat allows a hand to trail along the silken surface of the water, the woman allowed her mind to drift with the surface

of long past events. She had reached the butcher shop;
had almost gone by it.

"How do you do, Mrs. Farley? Nice warm weather
we're having." The butcher had a hooked nose and
when he smiled it seemed to press down his thick brown
mustache that framed his even white teeth so beauti-
fully. He settled his apron over his stomach and gazed
at her hungrily and affectionately above the glass top
of the counter as though he were trying to hypnotize
her into buying some of the coral pink sausages which
reposed beside a block of ice in the transparent case.

The meat shop was as white as death. It smelt of
blood and sawdust and its tiled interior offered a refuge
from the heat without.

"I want a piece of—can you give me a nice rib roast
today—? No! What do you ask for those hens?"
Mrs. Farley, as always, hesitated when she spoke and
lines as fine as hairs traced themselves on her pale, dry,
hastily powdered forehead. Her vague, rather squinting eyes traveled undecidedly over the big pieces of
meat: the shoulders, the forelegs, the haunches, of differ-
ent shades of red streaked with tallow or suet, that
swung on hooks in the shadow against the gray-white
tiling of the walls. The fowls dangled in a row a little
to the fore of the meat. The feet of the hens were a
sickly bluish yellow, and the toes, cramped together yet
flaccid, still suggested the fatigue which follows agony.
The eyes bulged under thin blue-tinged lids and on the
heads and necks about the close-shut beaks bunches of
reddish brown feathers had been left as decorations.
The butcher took one down and, laying it on the coun-

ter, pinched up the plump flesh between his forefinger and thumb.

"You could never find a better fed hen than that," he told her. "Nice firm solid meat. You see they are just in and I was so sure of getting rid of them I did not even put them on the ice yet. They're not storage fowls. I buy them from a young man who has a farm out near where my sister lives at Southbridge."

Mrs. Farley, in spite of a gala occasion and the fact that Mr. and Mrs. Price were to do her the condescension of coming to dinner at her house the next day, had not intended to buy anything so expensive as chicken. For all those people it would take two hens. But though she tried her best not to allow the butcher to catch her eye, she knew he was staring at her intently and that the white teeth were flashing almost cruelly under the brown mustache beneath the hooked nose. It heightened a conviction of weakness which she never failed to experience when she was called upon to decide anything, especially in the presence of other people, and she wished she had asked Alice to buy the meat before she went to work. Of course Alice would spend too much but what she got was sure to be nice and the diners were certain to praise it.

"I will take two of the hens," said Mrs. Farley, moistening the dry down along her lips. "Be sure you give me fat ones," she went on, frowning. While she fumbled in the pocketbook for the money she did not cease to be aware of the pleasant confident manner of the butcher, as with deft fingers he ran his hand into the bird and with a slight clawing sound tore out a heap of discolored entrails so neatly that not one burst. Then he slit the chicken's neck and extracted its crop. Mrs. Farley was anxious to get away. She never had any peace of mind except when she was by herself.

"I'm sure you will be pleased," declared the butcher with a slight bow, as he took the money she handed him. Her short white hand was corded with bluish veins and her fingers were slightly knotted and bent from gout. They had hovered almost palpitantly over her worn black purse while she tried to make up her mind whether to give him the exact amount or to ask him to change the five dollars which Alice had turned over to her that morning. At last she gave him the five dollars, and when he counted the sum due her into her palm the dull brightness of the pieces of money swam slightly before her eyes and she had no idea whether or not the amount returned to her was what was owing.

The butcher bowed again, managing to appear deferential. "Where shall I send them?" he asked, inclining his ear toward her, and in a low hurried voice she recalled the number he had forgotten. "They must be sent right away," she insisted, "or I can't get them ready." With a gallant inclination of the head the butcher promised to send them at once.

She made her way through the bitter-smelling gloom and as she pushed the screen door open a large blue fly rose stupidly and bumped against her face.

She was obliged to go to the grocer's and to the bakery and when she approached her home again it was already three o'clock in the afternoon. May, Winnie's little girl, an unhealthy looking child with lustrous wax-like skin, large, vapid, glazed, blue eyes, and thin, damp curls of gray-blonde hair which clung to her hollow shoulders, rose from the shadowed doorstep.

"Hello, Grandma," she called, with one hand smoothing the front of her faded pink gingham dress, while with the other she pressed her weight against the grimy iron balustrade.

Mrs. Farley's eyes frowned wearily but a conscientious smile came to her lips that were twisted a little with repugnance.

"Where's Mamma, May?" she asked, not looking at the child. "Is she lying down?" May sucked her middle finger and wagged her head from side to side. Her smile was vacant in its timorous interest. "Do you want to take one of my bundles?" May nodded her head up and down and accepted the parcel. Her small arm twined around it loosely. The front door was ajar, opening into a familiar smelling twilight, and she hopped after her grandmother into the house.

*   *   *

As Mrs. Farley entered the darkened bedroom, Winnie, in a cheap, fancy négligé of lilac and pink, rose from an old corduroy-covered lounge and came forward to meet her. Winnie's small, pointed face was haggard and smeary with tears. She gazed at her mother-in-law with a childish look of reproach.

"O Mamma Farley, I know Laurie will say some terrible thing again!" She wrung her hands that were plump through the palm and had tapering fingers which curved backward at the tips. "I have been lying here all afternoon worrying about what may happen to-morrow!" As she spoke she glanced beyond her mother-in-law's head to the heavily beveled mirror in the old bureau, and her rapt, tragic face became even more voluptuously tragic as it contemplated itself.

"Now, Winnie, I have talked to Laurence and he realizes perfectly well that he can't say what he thinks to your father. He will let bygones be bygones just like the rest of us."

"O Mamma Farley, you don't know Laurie! And he hates Papa and Mamma so and he has no mercy on me. Sometimes I think he hates me, too!"

Mrs. Farley's mouse-gray hair hung in straight wisps below the edge of her shiny old black velvet turban which was tilted askew. Her withered face became harshly kind. She had more firmness when she was with Winnie than in the presence of other people.

"You must remember, Winnie, that I have known Laurie considerably longer than you have. Pull yourself together and rest and don't worry about this any more. I know it will be all right."

May had followed her grandmother and now stood awkwardly and apologetically on one foot watching the two women. When her mother glanced at her, her face quivered a little. She looked at the floor and rubbed the scaled toe of her slipper against the raveled blue nap of the carpet.

"I am going to make a cake today." Mrs. Farley sighed as she turned toward the door. "There's my

usual Saturday baking, too. You'd better keep still
so you won't be feeling worse tomorrow. If I get
through in time tonight I'm going to press your yellow dress for you. I want you to look pretty." She
left the room.

Winnie was not sure that she wanted to look pretty.
She was a little ashamed of the feeling but she would
have liked to create with her parents the impression
that the Farleys had not treated her well. This was
from no desire to injure the Farleys but rather from
an intuition as to what kind of story of the past years
would please Mr. and Mrs. Price most and present
their daughter in the most interesting light.

May, sidling reluctantly toward the hall, still
watched her mother. Winnie's eyes, with soft, hostile
possessiveness, fastened themselves on her little girl's
face. May would have preferred not to meet her mother's eyes so straight.

"Come here, May!" Winnie sank suddenly to her
knees and held out her arms. May walked forward,
seeming not able to stop herself.

"You love Mamma anyway, don't you?"

"Yes," May said. There were bubbles of saliva on
her lips because she would not take her finger away
from her mouth.

"*You* don't think I'm selfish, May?" Winnie shook
May a little, then held the child to her. A shudder
ran like a live, uncontrolled thing between them.

May was ashamed of the shudder as if it had been
her fault. Winnie drew away and stared at her daughter. Winnie's eyes were soft and wistful with hurt, but

underneath their darkness as under a cloud May saw
something she was afraid of. It was angry with itself
and demanded that she give it something. She did not
know what to give it. To escape it she wanted to
cry.

Winnie wanted to make May cry but hated her for
crying.

"You *must* love me, May! I'm your mamma! You
must love me!"

"I do," May said. Her eyes were black with tears,
but because she wanted to cry she could not keep her
lips from smiling a little.

"As well as you love papa?"

May felt accused of something. She could not make
herself speak. She was sorry and wanted her mother
to strike her.

"Then you love Papa best? Oh, May, that's cruel!
You mustn't love him best!" Winnie's excited manner
was contagious. May did not know how to explain
what was the matter and suddenly burst into tears.
Winnie moved back again and watched the little girl
with her arm over her face, crying.

May's sobs lessened. Without knowing what had
occurred, she felt utterly subjugated. She wanted to
love her mother, but the soft, angrily caressing eyes
would not let her. When would her mother let her stop
crying? There were no tears any more. It was hard
to cry without tears.

"Poor naughty Mamma doesn't know what she's
done!"

May, with her eyes shut, stole out a hand which trembled on her mother's face.

"You do love me then? May, you must! You mustn't love Papa best!"

"I don't!"

They kissed. May saw that her mother's eyes were like things standing in their own shadows and loving themselves. They liked being sad. They yearned over May's face, but it was as if they did not see it and were yearning for themselves.

"Go play with Bobby then, dear, and don't hurt poor Mamma like that."

"I won't."

May ran out and left Winnie looking into the glass beyond where the child had been. Winnie could not understand how she could be blamed for anything. She was so innocent, so childlike. At one time Laurence had been able to discover no faults in her. She recalled the early months of their marriage and remembered that in those days whenever she had reason to think him displeased with her she made funny little pictures of herself with her hands over her eyes and, signing them "poor Winnie," left them under his plate at table where he found them at the next meal. A pang of hatred shot through her, mingled with the recollection of caresses, involuntary on his part. She felt a need for justifying her increasing hardness of heart and when she regarded herself sadly in the mirror she was reassured. It was as if in the way her tousled reddish curls shot back the light there was something that contradicted blame.

It was four o'clock. Through the window the sunshine on the row of houses opposite paled their red bricks to the purplish tint of old rose petals. At the end of the street where the square began bunches of raw green foliage floated with a heavy stillness above the smutty roofs steeped in light. Behind the bright yellow-green leaves the blue sky melted into itself as into its own dream.

Laurence came home early on Saturdays and Winnie decided to dress. As she opened the front of her négligé Bobby entered the room and made her hesitate. He sweated and panted, dragging his feet and lugging with both hands a small tin bucket filled with the dirt he had dug in the back yard. He was very fat. He wore overalls and there was dirt smeared in the creases of his neck under his firm chin.

"Bobby! How can you!"

"Dirt. Nice dirt," Bobby explained. Everything about him showed that he belonged to himself. His brown eyes were passively against his mother. Grunting laboriously, he stooped and began to empty the rich purplish earth on the clean-swept blue carpet. Winnie's eyes flashed.

"Don't you dare do that, Bobby!" She sprang toward him, trying to be angry.

He did not mind. He kept his fat shoulders bent to his task.

"Stop it, I say!" Only a few grains of the damp, dark soil remained in the bright bucket. She gripped his elbow. He glanced at her, his solemn eyes twinkling with a kind of placid malice. His grasp on the tin handle relaxed and he sat down very flat on his plump bottom. Winnie dropped down beside him and began to laugh. She could not have said why but she always felt flattered by his defiance.

"Now what shall I do?" she demanded. They stared at each other.

"I'm makin' a house," Bobby said. There were still harsh lights in his placid eyes. They made her ashamed and glad that she was his mother. Her heart beat very fast and, escaping from an emotion which perplexed and disturbed her, she threw her arms about him and buried her face against his cool ear and his moist, cool cheek. "Oh, you love me! You love me! I know you love me!" she crooned, rocking him against her. "You love me as well as you do Papa, I know you do."

Bobby wriggled. "Don't love Papa!" he said.

"But you must! You know you must." There was a sob in Winnie's voice. She was sick, she said to herself. That was why she wanted to be loved.

" 'Don't love Papa!' You must love Papa, but love Mamma, too! Oh, Bobby, poor Mamma!" Bobby tried to pull away again, but she had felt some one looking at them and she would not let him go. Bobby's breath was warm on her half bare breast.

She turned her head, guilty, and ready to cry with hatred of her guilt. Laurence was in the doorway. She knew he had hesitated there, but when she looked at him he walked straight forward past her with the air of having only just arrived.

"Hello," he said. "Glad you are up."

"Look what Bobby's done." She let Bobby go.

"Into mischief as usual, eh?" Laurence said. He walked to the wardrobe and hung up his hat. He had a short, bulky figure, the head and shoulders too big for the rest of him. He had thick brown hair, coarse and very slightly sprinkled with gray. His skin was ruddy but did not look fresh. As he walked with his swaying, awkward stride, he held his head forward and a little to one side. His coat sagged on the hips and was caught up toward the back seam. His hands did not appear to belong to him. They were short, disproportionately small, and very delicate.

"Bobby, you should be made to clean up," Winnie said.

Laurence came over and looked at the pile of dirt. "May——" was all Bobby said. He wanted to get away from his father. He ran out.

"He's made a mess, all right. Can I help you up?" Laurence leaned to her and she gave him her weak hands. She wanted him to feel them weak in his. His mouth twitched a little as he pulled her to her feet. She hated the furtive bitterness that was in all he did for her, yet it struck a self-righteous fire from her. She leaned against him. She was frail and plaintive. He seemed to stiffen against her softness. She loved herself wistfully, her eyes lifted to his face.

To marry her he had given up the prospect of a career in science. An expedition to Africa with one of his old professors had been abandoned. At that time he had finished college and was working for a scientific degree. She was eighteen.

Winnie felt herself still to be good, pretty, and sweet. She had a right to something beside this distant tenderness. She knew there had been times when simply a look, a glance, a word from her had carried him off his feet. After these occasions there were symptoms of self-contempt on his part. Yet he was proud of her, she was certain. Often, without his being aware of it, she had seen him betray to others a secret vanity in possessing her. Surely it was no disgrace to yield to her!

She had sometimes caught him staring at her abstractedly, yet with such unyielding curiosity that it made her shiver to remember it. She clung to him so that he could not look at her like that now.

"Do you feel well enough to dress for dinner?" Laurence asked.

"Yes, Laurie—I'll feel all right if——"

"If what?" He was always harsh when he joked.

She twisted the button of his coat. His eyes narrowed against hers as though he were shutting her out. His sweet, harsh lips smiled. He gave her a kiss and moved out of her arms, going to the window.

She was ill. The doctor had advised another operation. Without it she could have no more children. She would die. She looked at Laurence. He hurt her. The line of his back against her forced her into herself. It was a pain. But when she remembered what a serious state of health she was in most of her bitterness passed away from her. An expression of sweetness and resignation came into her face. Her gray-green eyes shone in tears under her reddish, disheveled hair. In her illness she felt superior to her husband and was able to love herself more completely.

"I heard from Mamma today again, Laurence," she began gently.

"Yes?" Laurence had hesitated before replying. She wanted him to turn round. He kept his gaze fixed on the street beyond the open window. A soft current of motion stirred the bright heavy air blue with whirling motes. She could see his hair slowly lifted. Past his head the sky was pale with light. The sunshine floated green-white from the dim quivering sky.

She kept watching his shoulders in the sagging coat. "I believe you had rather see me miserable all the rest of my life! Oh, Laurence, how can you! I can't hurt Mamma any longer even to please you!"

"To please me?" Laurence's voice was sharp and sarcastic, yet it did not reproach. She hated its tolerance.

"Of course I know I can't please you!" she said. She could not see his face and it was almost unbearable not to know whether he was smiling or not. She felt him going farther away from her because of her mother. It was cruel. Now whenever he did not want to touch her he said she was sick. She hugged her sickness but she hated him for talking about it.

"Now, Winnie!" He was facing her. "I've tried to efface myself as much as possible as regards your parents. If you weren't nervous and ill you would realize that the time has passed for reproaching me."

"Forgive me."

"There's nothing to forgive."

She was irritated because he would not forgive her, but she went to him and laid her head against his coat. A tremor shot through him when she touched him and she did not know whether she was agitating him in a manner complimentary to herself or not. But something in her hardened. He had no right to conceal himself.

"Oh, Laurie!" They were still against each other. She felt him waiting for her to lift her head. When people married they became one. She was conscious of feeling cruel, but it seemed to her that she had nothing to reproach herself with. "I cut myself on my manicure scissors to-day. You mustn't be stern with me." He could not help thinking what a common deceitful-looking little hand she had. He was sorry for her.

"What a tragedy!" His lips rested on the finger an instant without giving themselves. They quivered a little. An emotion that was unpleasant and at the same time exhilarating swept through her and seemed to lift her from her feet. She thought sadly and complacently of how much she had suffered for him already.

"Where is May?" Laurence asked suddenly. He felt that in kissing Winnie's finger he had committed himself to some unknown almost sinister thing. He resented the stupidity of his thought.

"Downstairs, I suppose." When he talked of May, Winnie was glad to leave him. She felt as if he were lying to her.

Laurence moved toward the door, his gross body large in the darkening room. Winnie seemed to know each detail of him as he passed into the dark hall. It

was painful to know him so distinctly. She tried in
vain to revive the blurred apperception of him which
she had had in earlier days. She wanted people to
see him as she had seen him then. His rocking walk
humiliated her and when visitors were present she tried
to inveigle him into sitting in an armchair where his
heavy handsome profile would be silhouetted against
the light, his awkward body at rest.

I don't think it is right for him to show an exaggerated preference for one child, she told herself.
He doesn't love May! He exaggerates his feeling for
her out of pique. Winnie could not forgive him for
being kinder to May than she was.

She found a match. Among the shadows the invisible sun made patches of bronze light. In the dark
the match flared like a long soft wound of flame. The
gas rushed out of the jet with a thick hiss and the
flame spread into a fan. It was a wing covered with
yellow down, blue at the quill. The wind sucked at it
soundlessly.

She walked to the window which the gas flame had
already made dark. The sky was green-blue. Bunches
of black leaves on the trees in the square cut the dim
fiery horizon into twinkling segments. A telegraph
pole rose up like a finger higher than the houses and
appeared to lean heavily against the quiet beyond.
Behind flecks of cloud putrescent stars shone as
through flecks of foam on an enchanted sea.

Winnie pressed her head against the cold pane.
Laurence, herself, old age. She would never be happy.
A peaceful vanity took the place of her unrest. She

realized an ethereal quality in herself which coincided with the whiteness of her little hands. She was aware of her hands, delicate and precious against her breast. Her breathing tightened. She did not want to remember the ugliness of the long illness she had had and to think of the operation which threatened her threw her into a panic. When people talked too much to her of death she only saw something ugly which she did not understand. She wanted to get away from it. She felt that she should not be forced to think of death. It did not belong to her. If people only loved her and allowed her to be herself she gave everything.

She turned away from the window and walked back to the mirror.

*   *   *

Alice was the last to reach home for dinner. She closed the front door briskly after her. Its thud was muffled and at the same time emphasized by the quiet of the empty street behind it. She whistled as she took off her hat. The tramp of her feet toward the dining-room was like a man's.

"Hello, Mamma Farley. Hello, Laurie! Glad to see you down, Winnie." She tweaked Bobby's ear.

"Hello, Aunt Alice!" His voice was thick. Like a small amused Buddha, he looked at her.

May thought Aunt Alice was not going to notice her, but Aunt Alice patted the little girl's head. May was terrified and relieved when the big hand brushed her hair heavily. She smiled at Aunt Alice, but Aunt

Alice did not see her. Then her face grew stupid
with perplexity again and her eyes were like two dark
bright empty things; and under her frilled apron,
though she tried to hold her chest in tight, you could
see her heart beat.

Mr. Farley, who had been upstairs, was the last to
enter the dining-room. When Alice saw him her homely
rugged face lit with peremptory condescending affection and she said, "Come and sit by me this minute,
Papa Farley. Your soup is cold. What do you mean
by being so late?"

Mr. Farley was always embarrassed by Alice's
officious regard, but he would not permit himself to
become impatient. He was a large handsome man
ten years younger than his wife. His hair was pre-
maturely white. There were heavy lines at the corners
of his mouth and one deep fold between his brows,
but otherwise his face was smooth and fresh. His lips
were compressed continually into a smile. He veiled
his disconcerted rather empty blue eyes under defen-
sively lowered lids. He gave a quick glance around
the brightly lit table.

"Winnie's improving. That's good."

"Yes. You look better," Alice observed to her sister-
in-law. Winnie made a little moue as she met the
cheerful but accurate scrutiny of Alice's eyes. Winnie
felt aggrieved by this clearness of gaze. In resenting
it she pitied Alice, who had coarse sallow skin and
large hands and feet.

"Winnie has every reason to be better. Her father
and mother are coming to dinner with us." Mrs.

Farley's conversation was always studiedly general.
Her voice was weak and toneless and a little harsh, but
she spoke carefully with an agreeable intonation.
While she talked, her stubby uncertain hand grasped
the hilt of a long horn-handled knife and the thin
flashing blade sunk into the brown crusted beefsteak,
so that the beautiful wine-colored blood spurted from
the soft pink inner flesh and mingled with the grease
that was cooling and coating the bottom of the dish.
She laid fat brown-edged pieces of pink meat on the
successive plates which she removed from a cracked
white pile before her. The boiled potatoes were over-
done and burst apart when she tried to serve them.
On the thin yellow skin which hardened over their mealy
insides there were greenish-gray spots.

"I'm glad, Winnie. We're all glad. No grievance
is worth hugging like this." Mr. Farley held his hand
to his eyes but he spoke determinedly. They all knew
how hard it must be for him to accede to a meeting
with Mr. Price. Laurence, Alice, and Winnie thought
of the unkind things which Mr. Price had said about
their family scandal at the time of the break, and wondered if he would refer to it again.

Mr. Farley liked to do hard things. If his resolution hurt him he kept it and was not afraid of it.
He was comfortable in the bare cheaply furnished
dining-room because he felt that if he had desired
happiness he might not have been there; and as he was
very punctilious in his duties toward his wife he was
able to relieve the oppressive sense of sin which he had
carried with him during most of his life.

Winnie and Alice were both watching Laurence. His face was bitterly impassive. On a former occasion he had insulted Mr. Price. His present resignation was full of disgust. Winnie felt that he was giving her to her mother.

"You're not eating, dear. I let the children stay up because you were feeling better. I thought we would celebrate." Mrs. Farley's eyelashes were whitish. She carried nose glasses fastened to a gold hook on the breast of the black waist she had washed herself and ironed so badly. She squinted when she smiled, yet her eyes did not look glad, but tired.

"I'm trying, Mamma Farley." Winnie's sweet mouth was tremulous. She was glad to feel it tremulous. How could Laurence give her over simply because her heart would not let her refuse her mother any longer?

Alice cut her beefsteak with brisk emphatic strokes. She took big bites and chewed them with an air of exaggerated relish. She felt herself to be the one person in the world who understood Laurence, but she knew that he feared and resented her understanding. He had always been saturnine and had lived his life alone. At college he paid his own way until he won a medal which entitled him to a scholarship. After this he devoted himself to research work in biology. Alice's imagination had never quite encompassed his impulse in marrying Winnie and it was still more difficult to understand why Winnie had committed herself. Even in the days of courtship Winnie had often fled in tears from her lover. She was ashamed of his deliberated vulgarities, though they piqued and invited her.

Alice could not comprehend it. Winnie and Laurence
had been secretly married. When the Prices com-
manded their daughter to leave her husband, Laurence
had withdrawn from the decision and told her to do
as she liked. She had not been able to make herself
leave him. She did not know that she wanted to. Her
parents had cut her off. Ten months later May was
born. Laurence took his scientific knowledge to the
laboratory of a manufacturer of serums and began
to make a living.

"I used up most of your five dollars on some hens
today, Alice." Mrs. Farley's conscience was heavy
with the sudden silence at the table. It merged into
her own inner silence and became the voice of herself
from which she was anxious to escape.

"Good."

"You work so hard, Mamma Farley. Don't!"
Winnie, not wanting Mamma Farley to work, felt sad
and nice again and justified before Laurence.

"I'm used to it." Mrs. Farley's mouth puckered
in a prim tired smile. The mouth was satisfied with
itself, so it drew up like that.

"Don't deprive Mamma of the joy of martyrdom,
Winnie," Alice insisted, laughing shortly. Mrs. Farley
kept her withered lips smiling, but her eyes, dull and
confused with resentment, felt covertly and bitterly for
her daughter's face. Alice ate, oblivious. Mrs. Farley,
with physical irritation, felt Alice eating beefsteak and
swallowing it half chewed.

"You leave Mother alone, Alice. Expend your be-
nevolent energies somewhere else." Laurence, his lip

twitching with repression, stared hard and smiling into
Alice's eyes. Her eyes were a sad brown, a little dull.
They were quiet eyes staring back unreproachfully as
though they understood the pain of his. Laurence
had a constant unreasoning impulse to defy Alice.

"Thanks," Alice answered with tired sarcasm.

"I don't need any one to look after me, Laurence,"
Mrs. Farley said, her voice cheerful, her mouth wry
and tight, her lids drooped.

Mr. Farley was restless. "Your mother is right.
We must give Mr. and Mrs. Price a royal welcome
tomorrow. We must put ourselves in their place.
There are two sides to everything and it takes a great
deal of determination to make the first overture.
They've done that. Now it's up to us." Mr. Farley
was always afraid that the incipient quarrel between
Alice and her mother would develop plainer propor-
tions. He did not see the group about him clearly, but
a helpless smile was on his face. In terror of their
unkindliness he showed them how noble he was.

There was another silence. Mrs. Farley could not
bear it.

"Has Mr. Ridge decided when he will leave for
Europe, Alice?" Mrs. Farley's knife and fork in her
weak hands clattered against her plate.

Alice was silent a moment. "He won't leave before
next month," she said. She was very intent on her
food. A flush went across her forehead like a burn
half under her stringy brown hair. Laurence gave
her a quick half-pleased glance of involuntary inquiry.
Winnie stared at her with soft sharpness.

"Does the doctor think his eyes will get well?" Mr. Farley asked, too clouded with his own concerns to be aware of the tension in Alice's face.

"He hopes so. It is nervous strain and overwork mostly. There was some sort of infection, but that came as a result."

"Then you'll have a vacation. He can't take you to Europe."

"No," Alice said almost angrily. "I know where I can get green things cheap, Mamma. That market on Smith Street."

"I see where Ridge has been attacked by all his radical friends. He seems to have most of the world down on him for that last book." Alice would not see Laurence's sneer.

"He's too good for all of them," she said sharply.

Winnie pursed her mouth. It was an effort not to laugh. To see Alice show feeling for a man like Ridge made one hysterical.

Mr. Farley was not thinking of Alice or of Horace Ridge. Again and again, as if in spite of himself, he allowed his gaze to rest on Winnie. His daughter-in-law disturbed him and if he could avoid it he never looked her in the eye. If he could keep from noticing the throats and breasts and arms of women he was usually all right. Then if he were obliged to see them clearly he wanted to weep with the pain of it and when tears again blurred his vision he was relieved. Marriage had been a failure. There had been, he felt, terrible things in his life. Sex had invariably placed him in the wrong, so sex must be the expression of a

perverse impulse. Tainted, as he considered it, like
other men, he struggled to exalt himself into a vagueness in which particular women did not exist.

Winnie despised him, but she would not admit it to
herself.

"I'm so glad to see you better! So glad!" Mr. Farley repeated irrelevantly, uncomfortable because he felt
the sweetness of Winnie's face too intimately.

"Thank you, dear Papa Farley." Winnie laid her
hand gently on his big fist resting on the table. He
withdrew his fingers, but as he did so gave her hand an
apologetic pat. Her little fingers felt to her like iron
under his big soft hand. She knew he was afraid when
she touched him. Vulgar old man, she said to herself.
She despised him so that she wanted to touch him again
out of her superiority. "Dear Papa Farley!" There
was helpless moisture in his eyes which he could not
keep from her.

"I have some work today. I'll forego dessert."
Alice got up with sudden awkwardness and pushed her
chair back. She smiled at them all, not seeing them.

When she had gone they were pleased and yet
ashamed of themselves, knowing why she went.

"Did you get your deal through, Father?" Laurence
asked impatiently after a moment. They were all relieved of the silence too heavy with Alice.

* * *

The window was open and the thick dark night, coming warm and moist into the bedroom, made Alice feel

as though some one breathed into her face, close against her, stifling her. The yellow gas flame rushed up from the jet with a stealthy noise. The street outside was still.

Alice sat down before her typewriter and stared at it. Suddenly her full breasts heaved. "Oh, my God!" She buried her face. Her blouse pulled tight across her shoulders as she stretched her arms in front of her.

Horace Ridge was going to Europe to remain two years. He might get well. He might die. His eyes. She felt herself lost in the darkness of his eyes.

Then something broke in her. I'll tell him. I'll go with him.

She dared not see herself in the glass opposite. Once she had abandoned herself to her desire to be beautiful. She remembered, with a horrible sense of humiliation, the hours spent behind locked doors when she had tried to make herself into something men would like. One day she had done her hair a new way, and, going into the living-room, had caught Laurence's ridiculing eyes upon her. That was before he married Winnie. Alice realized that something had gone wild in her. She had picked a paper knife from a table and hurled it at him and it had cut his hand. His face had turned scarlet, then white, then scarlet again. He had gone out as if he were glad, without speaking to her.

After that she fixed her hair the old way and avoided the mirror. She did not want to realize what she was. Nothing existed but work.

When she met a pretty woman in the streets Alice

had a sense of outrage. A self-righteous flame burnt
in her. Then she tried to be patient and it grew cool.
She wore heavy careless clothing. She was generous
to Winnie. Most of all it relieved Alice to buy presents for the children.

It was the evening before when she came home from
work that Bobby met her in the hall. Then there was
jam on his unperturbed face. "You donna bring me
sumpin'," he reminded her.

She held out a top. For an instant a cold gleam of
possession lit Bobby's still eyes in his fat face. He
grasped the top and moved a little away from her.
His air was suspicious. When he was sure the top
was his the cold light died from his face. He was
smooth and shut into himself again. He was like a
china baby. To get at his soul one needed to break
him.

"You like it, eh?" Alice demanded. Her eyes were
more violently hard than his. She seemed to like him
against her will. She bent down. His lips brushed
her cheek dutifully and she felt as though a mark had
been left there. She imagined it a spot like frost with
five points like a leaf.

"Tan I go?"

As he went away from her the spot burned her.

Inexorably Bobby descended to the back yard. He
seemed to know how futile a thing Alice was compared
to himself.

With her face buried on the oilcloth cover of the
typewriter Alice's thoughts, all confused, ran on God,
art, suggestions that had come to her as Horace Ridge

dictated his book. Then in the turmoil she could see
Horace Ridge's big figure still against the light of the
window where he worked. Alice felt herself light, clear
and vacuous, absorbed in the substantiality of this picture.

Christ died on a cross. She felt sick as with disgust.
Good to others. Hate. Winnie.

Alice could not bear to think of the children born of
Winnie. Bobby born of Winnie. She could not think
of him. Virgin Mary. There seemed something secret
and awful in maternity—some desecration. She felt
the child helplessly intimate with the mother's body.
He did not want her. Other religions. No time to
read up. Buddha. Sex. Marriage. Laurie was an
atheist. He wanted to be perverse.

Must be something. Nice pictures. Art. Beauty.

When she said beauty to herself her heart was hard
with resentment. Long-haired men. Rot. They did
not understand.

She cried a few moments thinking of nothing, but it
was as if something unseen grew strong with her weakness. It drank her misery and left her dry. She got
up, feverish, and stood before the glass, hating herself.
Her waist had pulled apart in front and she saw the
swell of her big firm breast. Her face was heavy
and ugly with rebellion, sallow, the eyes inflamed.

She saw her breast. Strange shiver of curiosity
about herself. Why did it hurt her to see her breast?
She covered it up.

She looked at herself, into her hot eyes. Something
cried inside her for mercy, but she would not take her

hot angry eyes from the face in the glass. No use to beat about the bush and pretend to be highfalutin'. Wanted what Winnie wanted. Disliked Winnie. She had a corroding sensation in her throat as though she tasted metal. Then shame mounted hot over her as though it were swallowing her. She resisted being swallowed. Her skin quivered against the hot cold engulfing sense of degradation. She was like a bird alive in a snake's body.

Something tightened in her soul, and the emotion she had experienced the moment before flowed away from her. Receding, it left a hardened accretion like petrifying lava flowing down cold from a volcanic crater.

Still she stared at herself. Homely woman. It seemed to her that her veins crept like snakes along her arms. Life stealing upon one through the veins. Stealthy life running red and silent in its bitterness through the body. Where to go to? Horace Ridge. He has any woman he wants. Famous man. Me.

She felt slightly intoxicated by a frank acknowledgment of her absurdity. Her horror of herself crept over her body, shameful because of no use.

I can't endure it!

Her wrist pressed against her teeth and made a mark, but no blood came. She wanted to tear away her flesh, but it seemed to resist her. It was full of hurt where her teeth had pressed. Life sucked at her like a wild beast.

She turned from the mirror and hurled herself face downward sobbing on the bed. Her body oppressed her.

She cried a long time. The work would have to go.
At last she crept off the bed and undressed herself and
put out the light, but she lay awake, and the darkness
remained electric and horrible. She closed her eyes
and tried to shut out its intimacy.

Mamma and Papa Farley. What was wrong between them? Sex. Horror. She tried to keep her
thoughts from integrating. Child. She bit her wrist
again and turned over in bed. Too proud to hate
Winnie. Other girls. Their faces opened against hers.
They were white and flowering in the dark. Eyes open,
waiting to receive men. She shivered. One must think
about these things. Winnie's maternity. Bobby seemed
slimed all over with Winnie. To wash Bobby clean—
clean of Winnie!

Alice was still awhile. She was dark inside, but the
dark grew calm. She began to go over things very
clearly. What was passion? Fourteen years old.
Pain. Words written on back fences.

I am glad to be out of it. Poor little Winnie.

Outside, cool. Cool ache of being outside life.

Horace Ridge's settled form, quiet against the dancing window. He turned in his chair. Kind eyes behind
glasses. He could keep people outside him because he
had all they could give him already there behind brown
agate eyes.

Albert Price—short trousers, face like a girl's. They
knew.

She, twenty-nine years old, outside their lives. She
did not want her body. If she could only make Horace
Ridge understand that she had no body! Clothes made

her virgin when she was a mother. If she could undress herself he would know that she was a mother. Clothes made him forty-three years old, radical critic of life and manners, ruined health, blindness incipient. She wanted to undress him to show him how little he was.

Oh, dear! She cried. It hurt, but less. Oh, dear! Life was a muddle. When one ceased to desire there was quiet, bitter and beautiful quiet. Laurence, Winnie, Mamma and Papa, far away from her—pathetic with distance. Horace Ridge far away from her. Her loving him cool. Nothing. She wanted nothing. Heart in the breast coolly melted like water in a still cup. In the bed in the darkness her still heart reflected the shadows of hot summer pavements, brick houses with fronts beaten flat and dull by sun, the moment before nightfall when lights burst from the theater fronts and the streets were gay with people in pale colored clothes. Then the heart was still, was cool—was water into which the darkness came gratefully covering the loneliness.

*   *   *

Alice was sorry for herself because she had a mother like Mrs. Farley. Poor Papa Farley. Alice loved him and despised him. She did not love her mother.

On Sunday when Alice went downstairs Mrs. Farley had on her gray taffeta dress and was intent on setting the house right. She walked stooped a little forward, her shoulders drawn together. The eyeglasses that hung on her chest twinkled. Short straight soft hairs floated, unpinned, at the nape of her neck. When she turned her head the withered skin made fine swirls of wrinkles about her throat. She walked very fast about the parlor putting the chairs in place. She took short steps so that her haste appeared feverish. The occasion seemed to fill her with a kind of worried happiness.

Mr. Farley had put on his frock coat. He had no dignity in it.

"Don't work too hard, Mother." He went into the dining-room smiling in bland anticipation of whomever should be there.

Alice was at table. She was ashamed of her red eyes and barely glanced up. "What would Mamma do if we forgot for one day to object to her working so hard?"

Mr. Farley spread his coat-tails and sat down on the oak chair with the imitation leather seat. Alice's remarks about her mother made him feel guilty.

"We should have gotten up earlier so your mother wouldn't have the dishes to worry about."

"I'm going to wash 'em," Alice said shortly.

It was a hot day. The clouded sky was a colorless glare. A thick wind stirred the ragged awnings upstairs before the bedroom windows. For a moment the sun came out as though an eye had opened. The house fronts were a pale bright pink. Dust made little eddies in the empty Sunday street. The awnings lifted, then hung inert like broken wings. When a wagon passed you could hear, above the rattle of the wheels, the muffled thud of the horse's feet striking the soft asphalt.

May was on the front steps. She wore a very stiffly starched white dress and a pink sash, wilted and wrinkled by many tyings. Her hair was brushed back very smooth and gathered away from her forehead with a flapping bow. Pale with interest, her small face turned toward the corner of the square as she watched for the Prices to come.

In the parlor, Winnie stood out of sight behind the freshly laundered curtains, and watched too. Laurence had left the house. She wondered if he were going to avoid her parents.

As the time passed the sun disappeared again and shadows flowed into the street which was as gray and still as water.

When the equipage with shining lacquered sides flashed into the empty place May looked at it bewildered, but Winnie had seen it through the window and recognized her parents.

The carriage drew up before the house and the wheels scraping the curb made a long rasping sound. The chestnut horses were fat. Their harness twinkled. They wriggled the stumps of their clipped tails against the cruppers that constrained them. On their breasts where the circingles had rubbed and on their flanks and buttocks the hair was darkened and matted with lather.

May was afraid and proud because the beautiful horses stood before her home. They stamped. A shiver ran along their satin bellies. Their breasts and forelegs quivered with tension as they jerked their heads in the check reins and pressed the street with harsh hoofs below their rigid ankles. Watching them, May uttered a little cry of terror and delight; but she thought some one had heard her and she clapped her hand over her mouth.

The footman had jumped from his place, and Mr. and Mrs. Price were descending from the carriage.

Indoors, Winnie felt her heart swell with a pain of pride. These were her parents. All these years she had been robbed of this!

"Oh, Mamma Farley! They've come! They've come! I thought I should never see them again!" Winnie's smooth fingers clutched Mrs. Farley's stiff nerveless palm. "What shall I do? It hasn't been my fault, has it, Mamma Farley?" Winnie's soft relentless gaze clung to her mother-in-law's face.

Mrs. Farley nervously desired to evade. Winnie made her feel guilty of the situation with which she had nothing to do.

"Now, dear! Now, dear! We won't talk about who's to blame. Could your mother have written the note she did if she intended to reproach you?"

"But Papa—— And Laurence hasn't come back yet! He and Papa will quarrel again! You shouldn't have let him do this way, Mamma Farley! Oh, feel my hands! They're so cold!" Her eyes, large and dark, shone with a languid and deliberate excitement. She wished that Alice were in the room to see her. Wry thoughts of Laurence. Resentment in Winnie's mind was like grit in something that otherwise would have moved oiled.

"What must I do, Mamma Farley? Shall I go to the door?" Winnie wrung her hands.

"I think you ought to meet her first. She would like to speak to you before the rest of us come in."

"Oh, I can't! How can Laurence leave me like this?"

Mrs. Farley, called on again to explain Laurence, made some meaningless gestures—clasped and unclasped her hands. Her fingers, pressed hard as they intertwined, made her knuckles glow white.

"Now, dear! Now, dear!"

"You *must* go with me! I can't bear it if Papa says anything to me about Laurence! What shall I do?" Winnie dragged Mrs. Farley across the brightly swept parlor carpet and into the hall.

May had already opened the front door. Mr. and Mrs. Price stood against the light of the street, their faces in shadow. Behind them the coachman was turning the carriage away. The footman sat very straight with his arms folded. The wheel spokes flashed. The polished black sides glistened.

Mrs. Price's flat face was very white above her elegant black dress. There were fine lines of strain under her pale eyes staring wide through her delicate pince-nez. The nostrils of her flat nose quivered a little. She had a thin narrow body and broad flat hips. She was breathing quickly. On her drawn lips there was a labored smile.

Mr. Price removed his beaver hat and revealed the top of his broad flat head, bald and bright, above his hard eyes which were like cloudy stones of pale blue. His thick under lip, thrust sullenly forward, showed under his thin yellow-gray mustache. There was no color anywhere about his face. Only under his chin where he had not shaved clean you might detect his beard by a colorless shining.

There was a moment of silence and hesitation. "Winnie!" Mrs. Price's voice shook. "Mamma!" They lay in each other's arms.

Mrs. Price's fragile hand moved uneasily over her daughter's hair.

Mr. Price, gruff and uncomfortable, his face unmoved, said, "Where do I come in?"

Winnie reached out and patted her father's arm. He took her hand. She kissed him, not wanting to. He made her think of herself. She wanted to relax in joyous agony. Lifting her soft strange eyes to her mother, Winnie was double, knowing, as before a mirror, how she looked. Sweet to have people unkind when you could forgive them!

But behind everything the recollection of Laurie intruded harshly.

In the background Mrs. Farley stood uneasily, and May, afraid to enjoy the family happiness, yet unable to leave, hopped from one foot to the other with subdued exclamations, her face alternately blank with confusion or atremble with response.

"Don't cry, Winnie, dear. We are all so glad, Mrs. Farley." Mrs. Price pushed Winnie gently aside and put out a frail hand, determined, though it shook a little. Mrs. Farley's fingers were clumsy, fumbling for Mrs. Price. Mr. Price shook hands in a fat abrupt fashion. They passed into the house.

"Not too much emotion. Not too much emotion,"
Mr. Price grumbled. May retreated before him won-
deringly. No one had noticed her.

Then Winnie said, "This is May, Mother."

They all stopped. May stopped inside herself.
"Dear!" Mrs. Price had kissed her. May knew the
kiss to be stale, dry, with a bitter middle-aged smell,
and was ashamed of knowing. The dry bitter kiss
drank of May's coolness. She was dumb under the
caress of the sick hand.

The parlor was clean and gloomy.

"Sit down, sit down," Mrs. Farley said. "I—
we——" She was trembling all over. She wept because of the rightness of things. "Such a glare!"
She tottered to the shade. Her silk dress rustled.

"There, Mrs. Farley. We're all right. An experience like this is good for all of us. Christ has taught
us to forgive our enemies and when we do I believe we
never have cause to regret it."

Mr. Price sat down awkwardly and coughed severely
into his mustache. His furtive gaze traveled malig-
nantly about the shabby room.

"How-d'ye-do, Mrs. Price? Mr. Price?" Alice
walked heavily in among them. Mrs. Price turned
around, disconcerted. Their hands touched. Alice
seemed to take charge of things. Mrs. Price suddenly
felt weak and was obliged to seat herself.

Winnie was annoyed. She went up to Alice plain-
tively. "Oh, I'm so happy, Alice!" She wept.

Alice was still, like a warm rock. "We're happy to
see you happy."

As Alice remained gruff and unmoved Winnie became more humble. "You don't look like it. Please let me be happy, Alice. I can't if—if——"

"Nonsense," Alice said.

Winnie smiled mistily at everybody.

"Come sit by me. I want to see my dear little girl." Mrs. Price disliked Alice, who remained hard and kind while Winnie cried with happiness. "You're not well, I know. Mrs. Farley wrote me. There, there. We must begin to take better care of you." Mrs. Price pulled Winnie to her. Winnie's eyes, rapacious with humility, were lifted again.

Mr. Farley came in, casting a rapid glance around the group. His smile was patient. Fear made him tired.

"Well, well—we're so—Mrs. Price." He stopped before her, not sure that she would shake hands with him. She gave him her finger tips and he took them miserably.

"Yes, I'm sure you all enjoy seeing Winnie happy," Mrs. Price said. She was cold and kind. Mr. Farley knew what she was thinking of—Helen out in Kansas City. They had spoken of the old scandal in objecting to Winnie's marriage.

"Mr. Price?"

"Hello, Farley. Hello." Mr. Price got up reluctantly. His hand clasp was a condescension.

Mr. Farley had given his hand limply. His mouth bent with acceptance. His smile was still tolerant but a little bitter, and he did not look up.

"Winnie comes first, Farley. Time to disagree about
other things later."

"I hope we are through with disagreements."

"Yes, Farley, I hope we are. Ahem."

Mr. Price sat down again abruptly.

"I'm so happy, Papa Farley!"

Winnie's eyes. He shuddered, trying not to see them,
fearful that he would forget to smile. "I'm glad you
are, dear."

Winnie clapped her hands and turned once more to
her mother. "Bobby! You haven't seen Bobby! Oh,
he's the dearest—— He's upstairs taking a nap."

Alice stood defiantly in the center of the gloomy
room, her feet apart, her stout hips set out. "Want
me to see if he's awake?"

"Suppose we all go out and leave Winnie alone with
her parents for a few minutes," Mrs. Farley suggested,
her voice quavering slightly. She puckered her lips
and frowned, smiling about her at the group. When
she stood up her gray taffeta dress settled slowly, with
a calm sound, in folds about her. The hem lay out on
the carpet. She had a scrap of yellow lace at her
neck and above it in her withered loose skin you could
see the flutter of a pulse.

"We certainly should," Alice said.

"Why, that's very nice. I don't——" Mrs. Price
looked around, uncertain, well-bred.

"Yes, yes. Come, May." Mrs. Farley took May's
small cold hand, moist in her dry one. Alice went first
and Mr. Farley shuffled after the others, head bent,
smiling, not sure why they were going out.

Mrs. Price had risen with her husband and stood, sad and calm, watching them leave. Life had wrung her, but she had grown sure in compromise. There was dignity in her sureness.

"Well," said Mr. Price shortly, "I don't see that husband of yours about!"

Winnie started tremulously. She smiled at him with a relaxed mouth. "Papa, dear, I know——" She gulped, still smiling.

"Yes, I know. I know. I suppose he's run away from us."

"He'll probably be in later, won't he, dear?" Mrs. Price's transparent smile was a thin shield guarding Winnie from her father.

Winnie tried to speak. Then she gave way and flung her white arms about her mother's throat. "Oh, M-mother!"

"There, there. I know."

"Confound him!" said Mr. Price very savagely, biting his mustache.

"Please, Perry!"

"Oh, that's all right. That's all right. I'm not going to lose my temper."

"Don't cry, Winnie. Sweet Winnie."

"What I want to know is whether that—whether he refused to meet us or not?" Mr. Price asked.

"Oh, Mother—Papa—I——"

"Don't cry, Winnie. It's all right. Your father has resolved to overlook things and if he can bring himself to do that about what has already happened this last little rudeness certainly won't matter."

"But he said he—he would come."

"He did, eh? And then went out."

"Now, Perry—please?" Replying to his wife's pale
smile, Mr. Price coughed ambiguously.

"You need never be afraid of your father conducting
himself in anything but a generous manner, Winnie.
I wish you might have been at church last Sunday
when he presented the new organ!"

"I know, but——"

"That's all very well, dear." Mrs. Price's voice had
a disappearing quality. It floated and drifted from
her lips and her words died away from her like the
shed petals of a flower.

"I want—I want you and Papa to let me be happy!
I—I—— Sometimes I think nobody's happy. Mamma
and Papa Farley are not. I——"

Above Winnie's bowed head Mr. and Mrs. Price exchanged glances.

"They don't deserve to be!" Mr. Price snorted after
a minute.

Winnie glanced up. Mrs. Price's face twitched with
worry.

"Now, Perry, dear, please? Remember! We decided not to speak of that again." She nodded toward
the closed door of the hall. "I suppose by now you
have heard all about Mamma and Papa Farley, Winnie
—all the things that worried your father so, that he
tried to tell you about when you and Laurence ran
away—but living here with them as you are, I think it
best for us to try to forget it. Mrs. Farley is a very

long-suffering woman and has borne her lot very patiently."

Winnie wanted to ask more. She hid her face again. Once Laurie———

"Laurence never talks of it, and you know before, when Papa tried to tell me, how it was—you wouldn't let him. What was it, Mamma?"

"Do we need to talk about it, dear?" Mrs. Price stroked Winnie's hair.

"It was the talk about the town. I don't see why she shouldn't hear it! I wanted her to know it all before so that she could understand my objection to such a match."

"But we never understood clearly how it was ourselves, Perry. You know when Winnie was married and you wanted to tell her I thought it was no fit topic for a young girl. I said———"

"Yes, I know you *said*, but if she had known all about the thing from the start she might have made a better match for herself. At any rate, she's old enough to hear things now."

Winnie looked up and stood away from her mother. "Please, Papa, Laurie———"

"Yes, Perry, it isn't right to Winnie. We mustn't feel this way about her husband."

Winnie's little face was hard and a small soft fire of malice burned in her eyes. Though she resented Laurence, she was with him against her parents. She would have exulted in making them feel his inexorableness. Because he was strong against them she seemed to feel herself inside his strength, corroding it with

her weakness. Mingled with her desire to swallow her
world was a vague terror of her loneliness when it
should happen.

"Well, that's all right, Vivien. I'll say nothing about
her husband, but that father-in-law of hers—— It
seems to me the more she knows about him the better!"

"Perry, but in their house!" Mrs. Price was weary.
Her smile seemed to hurt her. Her white hands shook.

Winnie was drawn up taut, cautious like a savage
on a spoor.

"Perhaps Father ought to tell me all of it," she said.

"But not now! Not here! You said you knew——"

"I did know there was some reason Mamma and
Papa Farley didn't get along. I knew there was a
woman——"

"Yes! That miserable woman he was entangled with
in that filthy affair. I don't remember whether I told
you that he tried to leave Mrs. Farley and live with
her. Helen—Wilson—something—Mrs. Wilson. The
husband had him up as co-respondent. Then they discovered she was going to have a child." Mr. Price
spoke gruffly and hurriedly in a low voice and chewed
his mustache.

Winnie trembled with excitement. Mamma and
Papa Farley. Laurie. She felt crafty and sure of
herself. Why had Laurie never told her all of this?
He did not like to have her speak of it.

"Perry, we can not! We must not! For Winnie's
sake!"

"Did Papa Farley and the woman have the child,
Papa?"

"Oh, Winnie," Mrs. Price protested, "how can you ask such things!"

Mr. Price, hands in pockets, rose on his toes and sucked his mustache in and out.

"They committed every sin which the flesh has been heir to since the fall of man, so I suppose they had a child too."

"You don't know?"

"I have it on very good authority that they did."

"The child, of course, was spirited away."

"And where did the woman go?"

"Out West. To Kansas or Texas. Something." Still he rose on his toes. The flavor of his mustache seemed to give him a peculiar relish.

"Oh, Papa, how awful! I didn't know it was as bad as that." Winnie dilated with her secret. A quick passionate resolution of triumph shot through her. Her eyes shone tragically.

"Winnie—my dear—you are in no state to hear things like this," Mrs. Price said. There was a light knock at the door. "Psh!"

Mr. Price started a little, but continued to elevate and lower himself on his toes and stare at the ceiling. Winnie clutched her hands to her breast.

"Come in." Mrs. Price lifted her trembling voice.

Alice's face in the doorway. None of them could look at her. Winnie met the face at last.

"Bobby's awake."

"Isn't that nice. Now I will see the dear baby."

"Yes, Mother. Come, Father." Winnie, with a high

dreamy expression of conscious pain, followed Alice
out.

*   *   *

The bedroom, dark, cluttered by too great an attempt at coziness, had grown a little shabby.   The
yellow shades were drawn under the lace curtains.   The
blue carpet showed here and there a warp of colorless
cords.   On the sofa the velvet and plush pillows were
embroidered with mottos and flowers.   There were a
heavy bureau, an old-fashioned bed, and Bobby's crib.
May slept in the nursery across the hall.

Bobby, his eyes still opaque with sleep, sat upright
in bed, a dreamy look of disapprobation on his face.

Mrs. Price could say nothing for a moment, then,
"How lovely!   How lovely!   What a beautiful healthy
child!"

Winnie caught him in her arms.

Mrs. Farley moved forward, feebly shocked.   "He's
too heavy!   Oh, you mustn't do that, Winnie!"

Winnie turned and gave him to her mother.   Bobby's
fat body was sodden and relaxed in his grandmother's
arms.   Mrs. Price's resigned hands moved over him
agitatedly.   "He's so beautiful!"   Feeling ashamed,
she knew not why, she kissed him.   "Look, Perry!"

"Fine boy," said Mr. Price.

Winnie danced about.   "I knew you'd think so."

Mr. Farley waited sheepishly, approving with his
patience.

"We're all proud of him," said Alice shortly.   Mrs.
Price glanced up with a start.   "He's a fine grand-

son," she declared after a minute. There was something defiant in the way she stroked his hair, but she remained very gentle and ladylike.

May stood to one side, quivering. She wanted them to see her but, for fear they might send her away, kept very quiet. When Bobby did not want to be petted she was uncomfortable and when he liked it she was happy too.

*   *   *

Laurence had come into the house and, finding the lower floor deserted, had gone upstairs. He stood in the bedroom doorway. Winnie saw him first. She was disconcerted for a moment. A little shiver of excitement went through her. But she recovered herself as she gazed at him and felt small and strong.

"Laurie!" She made a cooing sound of pleasure. She turned to her mother. "Oh, Mamma, I want you and Laurie to hug!"

Mrs. Price's face was stained with faint color. She grew brittle and tense in her uncertainty. Holding Bobby on her arm, she put her hand out. It was as if she put her hand between herself and Laurence. "I hope we both love Winnie enough to overlook things," she said.

"I hope so, Mrs. Price," he agreed, coming forward, his lids drooping as if to shut out the painful sight of them all. He smiled in shame. They shook hands.

"Now, Papa!" Winnie led her father forward by his coat sleeve.

"How-d'ye-do, Farley? How-d'ye-do?" Mr. Price

was bluff and reluctant. Their hands barely touched. Laurence kept his glance on the carpet.

"Now I am so happy!" Winnie clung to her husband's arm. Her softness sank into him. He felt that if he lived he must harden himself against it. When she finally freed him he drew a deep unconscious breath. Then he forced his somber eyes full on Mrs. Price's face. "I am thankful, for Winnie's sake, that you and Mr. Price made up your minds to this," he said.

"We won't reproach ourselves with the past, Mr. Farley," Mr. Price interrupted. He would not allow his wife to be addressed in lieu of himself.

"I've never reproached myself, Mr. Price," Laurence answered coldly. Still he looked away.

"I don't doubt it, Mr. Laurence Farley! I don't doubt it!" Mr. Price's manner was full of secret scorn. He rocked on his toes and sucked his mustache ends again.

"The babies are dears," Mrs. Price said. "Bobby is wonderful."

Laurence regarded Bobby. "Sit up. Hold your head up. Don't act as though you were half asleep."

"Don't be cross with him, Laurie!" Winnie pouted. Laurence was torn. He must refuse to praise Bobby as the Prices praised him. Laurence felt that he could not protect his child against the approbation of his enemies. May sidled up to her father. When she touched him he did not look down at her, but put his arm about her. He held his shame of her close in his heart like a wound that he would not let be seen. He stroked her hair.

"Bobby is too heavy for you, Mrs. Price," Mrs. Farley protested, coming forward with an air of furtive protest.

"No, no!" Mrs. Price, exaggeratedly polite, held him closer and smiled. The smile made Mrs. Farley helpless. Mrs. Price knew it.

Mr. Farley had been outside the group. Now he moved nearer Mrs. Price and, leaning forward, shook Bobby's inert fist. "You like your old grandad, eh? You like your old grandad?"

Bobby scowled on them all and put his thumb to his mouth.

"What did I tell you about sucking your thumb?" Laurence demanded sternly.

Winnie's sweet eyes, covert with knowledge, gloated on her husband's face. "Don't be cross to him, Laurie, when everything's so nice."

"Stop sucking your thumb." Laurence took Bobby's thumb down from his mouth.

"For Heaven's sake, leave him alone. You'll nag him to death. All this ohing and ahing is enough to drive him to something worse than sucking his thumb," Alice said shortly.

Laurence gave her a swift contemptuous glance of anger, but controlled himself. "That's a good boy," he said more kindly as Bobby lifted himself straighter and stared around.

"Oh, everything's so nice! I was so afraid it wouldn't be!" Winnie sighed again with happiness. Laurence passed his hand over his eyes, the delicate hand that, below the coarse sleeve of his coat, was like the revelation of a secret.

"You didn't think your husband was going to refuse to shake hands with me, I hope?" Mr. Price demanded. His unsmiling joviality was terrifying. No one could ever say exactly when he became serious and he was perfectly aware of the tremors of uncertainty that stirred in his hearers. He enjoyed disturbing them.

"We are exercising mutual forbearance," Laurence put in quietly. In the irritation of Mr. Price's presence something was slipping from Laurence's grasp. It was only half-heartedly that he continued to hold himself.

"Forbearance toward me! I hope you don't think I want you to exercise forbearance toward my religious views, young man! Has he come to his senses since you married him, Winnie?"

Winnie smiled feebly. Laurence looked at the floor. His lip twitched.

Mr. Price seemed to wish to drown out the echo of his words in the ears of those present and began to talk fiercely to Bobby. "Fine child. Father not going to raise you up to be a prizefighter, is he? Wouldn't surprise me. I hope your mother'll bring you up as a Godfearing man. She mustn't leave your education regarding the next world to your father. You'd better take him in hand, Winnie." He stared at his daughter with his vague hard eyes.

Laurence felt his parenthood raped. "Winnie and I have come to a perfect understanding regarding Bobby's education," he sneered.

Mr. Price glanced up at Laurence. "Have, eh? Ain't you an atheist? Last time I talked with you, didn't you tell me you were an atheist?"

"I did, Mr. Price. I'm afraid I am deficient in tact." Smiling, Laurence lifted eyes in which the light of hate was drawn inward toward some obscure point of agony.

Mrs. Price set Bobby on the floor. His legs were stiff with being held and he made a few steps away from her uncertainly like a drunkard. "The dear child!" she murmured uneasily. Her quiet smile was over her face like the still surface of a pool filled underneath with little frightened fish.

"Tact, eh?" Mr. Price was not sure what the remark meant, but, to give himself time, permitted a knowing twinkle to creep into his eyes. He rose on his toes. "If you'll leave off trying to set up science in the place of God we'll overlook your lack of tact," he conceded finally.

Laurence bit his lips. He assumed an irritating air of indulgent amusement. It was irresistible. He dared not look at Winnie. "I've sworn to preserve a reverential silence in regard to all of your pet fallacies, Mr. Price."

"My pet fallacies, eh! The years haven't taught you respect for the opinions of your betters, then?"

"I've never met them," Laurence said. Mr. Farley coughed. Mrs. Price had called Bobby back and was talking to him in a low tone, very intently. Mrs. Farley talked to Bobby too. Alice made with her tongue a clicking sound of impatience. Laurence had moved away from May. She watched the men in con-

troversy. Her mouth hung stupidly open. She had a
shivering white face and her eyes were all pupil. She
looked as though she had drowned herself in the darkness of her own eyes.

"Please, you two!" Winnie laced and unlaced her
fingers.

"You haven't? You know when you're in the wrong,
do you?"

"On the rare occasions when that happens," Laurence said with an ostentatious affectation of good
humor.

"And you haven't found out yet that you're com-
mitting a sin when you set yourself up in opposition
to Divine Truth! You're very complaisant, young
man! Very complaisant! But I'll tell you that Natural Science is out of date. The Darwinists and
Haeckelists and the rest of the dirty crew have to come
crawling back to the Creator they denied, with their
tails between their legs."

"You're making a dangerous admission in acknowl-
edging such an appendage, Mr. Price." Smiling at the
floor, Laurence reached out and drew May to him
again. He defied them with his loyalty to her.

"Am I? The devil had a tail before he ever heard
of Darwin, seems to me!" Mr. Price was still uneasy,
but swelled a little with the readiness of his retort.

"Laurie!" Winnie patted Laurence's sleeve, her
voice humble.

The humility in her voice inferred something in him
which outraged his self-respect. "And I haven't a

doubt that as in the present case the ass had ears!" he said sharply.

Winnie began to cry.

"I'll go, Winnie," he told her. It was inevitable. He had been that way before with Mr. Price. His hand fell from May's shoulder. He walked out. In the silence the group could hear the thick beat of his feet as he descended the carpeted stairs, and the reverberation of the front door which he slammed as he passed into the street.

Mr. Price's face was a dull red. He puffed out his cheeks. "That's what it comes to!" He shrugged his shoulders unutterably and turned with a gesture of departure and dismissal.

"Please don't go, Father!"

Mrs. Farley was wringing her hands. As May watched she seemed to be weeping from her own eyes her mother's tears.

"For Heaven's sake, don't take Laurence seriously, Mr. Price," said Alice.

Mr. Price lifted both hands with the palms out. "I don't! I don't! God forbid that any one should take that foolhardy blasphemy seriously."

Mr. Farley passed his hand over his face as though to brush away a cloud. His eyes were uneasy, his smile one of apology. "Laurence will regret it as soon as he is in the street."

"Regret! Regret's not the right emotion to recall that kind of talk. I take no account of what he said to me, but no one can go about in contempt of the God who made him and not suffer for it."

"I know——" Mr. Farley hesitated. His lips quivered a little.

"Oh, I knew I couldn't be happy!" sobbed Winnie.

Mrs. Price took her daughter in her arms. "Now, dear, your father has made up his mind to be forbearing. He won't go back on his word."

"No, I won't go back on my word, but I don't know whether I can ever bring myself to the point of coming into this house again. Not when that man's here."

"You oughtn't to take Laurence seriously, Mr. Price," Alice repeated. "I think we ought to forget about him and not spoil Winnie's day."

"I can't forget about him, Alice!" Winnie lifted her head indignantly from her mother's shoulder. Deep in her imagination Winnie, in a lace nightdress, was putting her arms about Laurie's neck. Her veins swelled strong and taut with confidence. She resented the injustice of being forced to choose between Laurence and her parents. Because of other things she could not forgive she would pardon him the day's scene, but she would not pardon her parents yet.

"It's all right, dear. Miss Farley don't mean that. She only wants us to forget the things your husband said to your father and I think that is exactly right. After he considers it I am sure he will come to the conclusion that he acted wrongly and be sorry too."

"I've had so much trouble," Winnie went on.

"Come, Bobby, let us all go downstairs and play games and help Mamma to forget her troubles." Alice jerked Bobby's hand. Leaning on her mother, Winnie followed. Mrs. Farley, her eyes red-rimmed with

unshed tears of perplexity, shambled after, her dress
rustling and disturbing her desire for self-effacement.
Mr. Farley descended the stairs with finger tips gliding
along the rail, smiling the abased smile of a blind man.
May, hesitating on each step, dragged unnoticed a long
way behind.

*   *   *

In the early morning the cloudy air had a texture
like wet wool. The sky radiated colorless heat like a
pool of warm water which one saw into from the
depths. Work had not yet begun on the corner house,
but in front of it dangled platforms suspended from
pulleys. The vacant windows smeared with paint gave
the house the look of a silly face smeared with weeping,
an expression of tortured immobility.

Alice, on her way to work, had just emerged from
her front doorway. As she descended to the street she
watched ahead of her a tall, very thin woman in a worn
silk blouse and an old skirt that still smacked of an
ultra mode. The woman dragged beside her a very
little boy in tight pants and a gay shirt. The little
boy, swinging by her hand, leaned heavily away from
her to pull a small red wooden wagon after him.

When the woman turned her head Alice saw her
bright blonde hair combed in glossy and salient puffs,
a cheap and unconscious defiance above her wasted
face and her breasts, sucked dry on her flat body.

Alice walked after her. Life. Thinking of money.
In the hot bed they touched each other. Rent due.
The child began to cry.

Old maid barricaded behind ridicule. Coolness of being outside. Loneliness like a cool wound.

The woman went on. Taller, narrower in distance, with her long limbs and graceful stoop she resembled a sculptured angel. Tomb. Apartment. The woman walked before Alice into a narrow marble doorway. The stone rolled back and the angel went into the tomb. Haggard and bitter face. A little rouge put on carelessly. Despair. No one knows why.

*   *   *

Laurence had come in during the night and gone to sleep on the box couch without disturbing Winnie. In the morning she was the first to awaken.

It had rained before dawn. The hot sun floated outside the window in voluptuous mists. The white curtains seemed stained with the pinkish-brown light. They swayed and parted and between their folds the moist air flowed heavily from the steaming street.

Winnie could hear the staccato tap of a hammer on the house next door. Horses' hoofs rang on the asphalt with a flat sound.

The curtains opened like lips and made a whispering noise. Then Winnie could see the wet bronze roof opposite shining blankly against the faint bright sky.

The room was crowded with the atmosphere of two people who have quarreled. They were oppressed by their consciousness of each other. Through the darkness of his shut lids Laurence, only feigning sleep, tried to ascend above the close room and his almost intolerable awareness of Winnie's presence.

She had seen his lids flutter. Tired and sweet, she regarded him mercilessly. She could see how tense the lines of his body were under the couch cover he had drawn up over his feet. His lids, pressed tight together, twitched a little.

"Laurie!"

With a helpless feeling, he opened his eyes.

Winnie's heart beat combatively, triumphantly. "I've been lying here looking at you," she said, her plaintive pout begging him to infer everything. "Bobby's still asleep."

Bobby lay in his little bed relaxed like a drowned child. His lips were pale. His face damp with the heat. His shock of blonde hair fell back on the pillow away from his head. Winnie, beside her big baby, abandoned herself to a sense of dependence which she felt him to justify.

"Yes? I must have slept very hard." In an effort to hide his surprise Laurence responded quickly to her overture. He sat up, smiling elaborately, and began rubbing his eyes.

Winnie would not let him escape through such casualness. "Are you still angry with me, Laurie?" She lifted herself among the pillows and rested on one elbow. There was a terrible youngness about her soft, hungrily uplifted face, her thin neck, the collar bones showing below her white throat. Her eagerness was too vivid. He was conscious of her rapacious youth. It made him tired. Youth demanding of him life and more life. Winnie was ill, but there was no rest for them even in her pain. He felt old and afraid of her,

as though he would never be able to get up from the
couch.

"Angry with you? Was I angry with you?" He
covered his eyes. His lips, smiling below his fingers,
were deprecating. He stood up slowly and lifted his
trousers from a chair. He felt ridiculous to himself
putting them on.

"Laurie? Please? Don't be angry with me for
wanting to see Mamma!"

He was hurt without knowing how she hurt him.

"Please kiss me, Laurie, dear! Don't be angry! I
can't bear to have you angry with me!" Her eyes,
strangely defenseless, opened softly to his. Their softness enveloped him and drew him down against the
harsh little sparks of reserve that burnt in their
depths.

"Kiss you?" he said. He took her fingers in his and
kissed them. His lips were grudging. He still smiled.
"Don't accuse me of being angry with you, Winnie. I
want you to have your mother back."

"But I want you, too. Kiss me! *Really!* Not like
that."

He leaned forward and his lips brushed hers. But
she would not let him go. She was so slight, pulling
him down, that he could not resist her. She pressed her
mouth hard against his face.

"Don't be angry with me."

"I'm not angry—wasn't angry." Each word was a
little shake to loosen himself from her.

"You won't talk to Papa that way again?"

"I won't give myself the opportunity. I won't see him again."

"Oh, Laurie!"

He withdrew above her, making himself paternal. "You must be sensible about this thing, Winnie. It's all right. I want you to see and be with your parents. If I avoid them it will be only for your sake. You're not well, Winnie. You're a little unreasonable."

"I can't bear being sick! Oh, Laurie, I won't be operated on! I can't bear it!" Her voice was passionate. She shrank, looking smaller among the big pillows. He pushed her into the limbo of invalidism. She did not know how to get out. His kindness was a wall between them.

He smoothed her hair. She was crushed under his tolerant hand smoothing away curls from her tear-wet face. "Shall I tell Mamma Farley you are ready for your breakfast?"

She gazed at him. Her eyes hurt him. They stabbed him through the silence she made. "Laurie, I think we are going to be so happy and then all at once when you talk about my being sick you seem so far away. You do love me?" She clung to his arm.

"Of course."

"Then kiss me again." He kissed her. Her terrible hunger hurt and confused him. He would rather not have seen her thin throat that suggested a young swan's, her pointed chin, her eyes, and the reddish hair which had slipped in confusion about her shoulders. The room, filled with her knick-knacks, choked him— her clothes on a chair, some soiled satin slippers, the mirror from which she seemed always to shine, her child asleep—hers and his together. He could not explain himself—felt that he was growing hard. He was ashamed of not loving her enough. Ashamed of the strength it gave him to know that he was not for her— now—that her health was keeping them apart.

"I want us to be happier than anybody, Laurie! Your father—you never talk to me about it! That woman out West who had a child by him! It's so— so terrible!" She felt his resentment of her persistent reference to it. There was something drunken in her which made her sling out words that were not wanted. She regretted a little this waste of her hoarded knowledge, but at the same time she was glad. He did not want to talk of it. She felt injured because he did not want to talk to her of it. She leaned against him. The tears ran from her blind uplifted eyes.

"That's nonsense, Winnie. What have we to do with them? I want you to be happy, too." He sat down beside her. She felt hopeless, as though she had lost him.

"Not just me, Laurie. Both of us."

"Of course. Both of us."

She was crushed. "You didn't know I knew all about your father, Laurie."

"No. I never told you the details, because it didn't seem worth while."

"You never tell me anything—not about yourself— or anything."

"I didn't think I could tell you anything about myself you didn't know already."

"Don't joke! I want you to love me."

"I do love you."

She was tired. She buried her face in the pillows. He rose from the bed and put on the rest of his clothes, but when he said good-by to her she would not answer him. He outraged the essence of her sex. She was weak. She wanted him to be weaker than she. She felt that he owed it to her. It was a crumb from his strength, she felt, to be weak to her who had to be weak to the whole world. She would not forgive him.

*   *   *

Laurence went out of the room, out of the house. A pale fiery mist rose up from between the houses and filled the wet morning street. The houses with lowered blinds were secret and filled with women. Girls going to work came out of the houses like the words of women. Women going to market passed slowly before him with their baskets. Pregnant women walked before him in confidence. The uncolored atmosphere threw back the sky. It was the mirror of women. Laurence felt crowded between the bodies of women and houses. He walked quickly with his head bent.

On the concrete pavements, washed white as bones by the storm of the night before, were rust-colored puddles. Dark and still, they quivered now and again, like quiet minds touched by the horror of a recollection. The reflections of the houses lay deep in them, shattered, like dead things.

*   *   *

Mrs. Farley stumbled up the dark stairway. Her knotted fingers with their tight-stretched skin kept a tense and fearful grasp on the scratched rim of the lacquered tray. On the clean frayed napkin she had put one of her best plates and on it rested a bloody peach and a dull bright knife. The peach, balanced uncertainly, rolled a little as Mrs. Farley moved. The knife clinked. Black coffee beaded with gold turned to saffron when it poured over into the saucer. The toast, burnt a little along the edges, slid back and forth in the napkin which enfolded it.

She stopped before Winnie's room. "Winnie!" Her voice sounded cracked with fatigue. With the tip of her black slipper, which was rough and gray with wear, she pushed the door back. The room opened bright before her. Her smile grew hard and solicitous.

Winnie sat up straight among the creased pillows against the dark old headboard. Her eyes were red. She smiled, too, and was consciously brave.

"Good morning, Mamma Farley! See how you have worked for poor little no-account me! Put the tray down and let me kiss you."

"Bobby isn't awake?" Mrs. Farley asked, embarrassed by her own pleasure as she pressed bitter and grateful lips to Winnie's firm cheek.

"Are you glad I was happy yesterday?"

"I hope you are happy today. You know how glad we all were."

"I want to be happy, Mamma Farley."

"And you will be, Winnie." Mrs. Farley set the tray shakily on the tossed bed clothes.

"You, too, Mamma Farley, dear. I want you to be happy, too." Winnie held out a small inexorable hand, and Mrs. Farley, unable to behave otherwise, took it. Winnie squeezed her mother-in-law's fingers. "I know you haven't always been happy, Mamma, dear." Winnie's dim eyes were lustful with pity. Mrs. Farley was frightened. Her hand trembled and she tried to pull back and resist the invitation of sympathy. "Papa Farley ought to love you more than anybody in the world!" Winnie asserted, passionately tender.

Mrs. Farley was shaken. Who's been talking to Winnie? She pressed her lips quiveringly shut. Her eyeglasses twinkled and shuddered with her heaving breast. Winnie felt herself strong with a love that nothing could resist. Exultant, she gloated inwardly over the knotted hand that trembled in her grasp.

"Your parents—I don't know—we won't talk about old people's troubles, Winnie." Mrs. Farley was recovering herself. Perhaps Winnie didn't mean that. "I suppose Papa Farley loves me in his way just as you love me in yours."

Winnie would not let her go. "You stand up for him. You're so good to him," she insisted with a kind of worshiping commiseration.

"Why shouldn't I be?" Mrs. Farley dared, trying to smile while she frowned, her evasive eyes shifting a little.

"Because he don't deserve it! Because he did what he did. Oh, Mamma Farley, I know you don't want me to talk about it, but I can't help it. I love you so. You're so wonderful to me!" Winnie's eyes shone, mercilessly sweet, into the hunted eyes of the elder woman.

"I don't know what you mean, Winnie."

They looked at each other. Mamma Farley could not look. She picked at the sheet.

"You dear! You dear!" Winnie hugged her. She was crying.

Again they leaned apart and regarded one another. Mrs. Farley's inflamed, withered eyelids twitched.

"Do you think Laurence really loves me? I'm so afraid!" Winnie said suddenly.

"Of course, Winnie."

"Oh, Mamma Farley, I want to be happy. I couldn't bear it if Laurence——" She buried her face in Mamma Farley's dress. Mrs. Farley stroked her hair.

"We're all foolish when we're young, but God is good to us. When we grow old we can have a little peace. But you're young enough—even for the kind of thing you want." Her pale mouth had a shriveled look of bitterness. "Love between men and women— the love you are thinking about—is not much in life, Winnie."

"But I couldn't bear not to have—not to have anybody love me."

"Look in the mirror. They'll love you." Mrs. Farley's eyes in her wet, wrinkled face were hard with contempt under the seared granuled lids.

Winnie, lying back, gloated over the thin white hair, the lined flaccid cheeks, and the eyes that glowed with weeping. Winnie swam in the strength of love like a swimmer sure of himself in trusted waters. She was grateful to the age and ugliness which did not claim her.

Mrs. Farley did not want Winnie to gaze at her any more. "Look! Bobby's awake," she said.

Winnie was satisfied and ready to be glad of Bobby, too.

The child sat up drunkenly. His touseled hair, matted with sweat, lay dark on his brow. His eyelids were pale and swollen with sleep. He rubbed them with his fists.

"Children are the surest happiness," Mrs. Farley said.

Winnie was oppressed. "I'm so afraid of being sick, Mamma Farley."

"You'll soon be well, I hope." Mrs. Farley had an air of resolution and dismissal. She went squinting to the crib. "My, what a sleepy boy!"

Laurie. Love. Children. Winnie had a terrible sense that she was losing some unknown thing which was precious and belonged to her but of which she was afraid.

"His night drawers are too small. His grandmother'll have to make him some. There's some nice stuff at that store next to the bakery."

They talked of shops. The atmosphere of the room seemed to lift with the lightness and sureness of their talk. They were safe and at rest among unchanging irrelevances. Women knew best the sureness of trifles. These were the things which did not change—which men could not change.

* * *

Late afternoon. There was no sun. Below the blank
gray sky, the long blank street. Along the street a
pair of sleek and ponderous black horses, with thick
manes and shaggy fetlocks, plodded before a loaded
dray. Their bodies rocked and swayed tensely with
strain. Their huge feet clattered and strove against
the asphalt. The hands of the driver, red, with full,
knotted veins, hung loose between his knees, holding
the slack reins. His body, in a khaki shirt, was
hunched forward miserably. From his fat stupid face
his eyes glanced dully under a bare thatch of neutral
tinted hair. Only the horses, purposeful and immense
in their obedience, seemed to understand.

In the gutter a street-sweeper, mild and tired, pushed
dry ocher-colored manure into heaps. Again and again
he stooped and lifted the shovel and the manure fell
into a cart. He wore ragged white gloves too large
for him. He was patient, but his gaze roamed, vague
with speculation. Servant of the horses that dirtied
the street, he was less sure than they.

At the corner house work was over for the day. The
abandoned platforms of the painters dangled loosely
on the long ropes. Through the smeared window-
panes you saw empty rooms blank as the faces of idiot
women waiting for love.

Alice walked slowly home from work. She saw her
own windows where the awnings did not stir. Drooping,
they cast their scalloped outlines vaguely into the
depths of the shadow-silvered glass. May was on the
front step.

"Hello, May." Aunt Alice's voice, very gruff.

May sucked her finger and ducked her head sidewise, smiling. Her finger slipped out of her mouth with a plop. She put it back between her wet lips.

"Coming in?" Aunt Alice held the door back. May went after her into the hall that was full of the smell of baking bread. Aunt Alice threw off her hat and walked, heavy-footed, into the living-room. May trailed after her in limp timidity.

Winnie, in her lilac négligé, sat in an armchair. "Oh, Alice. I've been talking to the doctor again and he's so horrid. He says I should have been operated on right after Bobby was born and now I'm getting worse."

Alice stood beside the chair and stared down. "Doctors like to croak."

Winnie reached up and clutched Alice's square dark hand. Winnie's white fingers were little claws digging into Alice's swarthy flesh. "Say I don't have to! I can't, Alice! I can't!"

"Well, I certainly wouldn't until I got into better shape nervously than you are now."

"Mother wants me to go away with her and I don't dare. I know it would do me good but I don't dare, Alice." Winnie half sobbed.

"Don't dare? What rot! Why shouldn't you dare?"

"Laurie will hate me if I go off with Mother! It doesn't matter how sick I am, he will hate me!"

"Winnie, you're talking the most unmitigated nonsense."

"I'm not, Alice. You don't know. He can't forgive me for wanting to be kind to Mother."

"I haven't noticed any signs of unforgiveness on his part. I admit he acted like a fool on Sunday but I suppose he can't be blamed. Your father's not the easiest person in the world to get on with, himself."

"I know, but you don't understand. Sometimes I think Laurie hates me for being sick. He don't love me any more! I know he don't."

"Laurence hate you for being sick! Good God!" Then Alice added, "You shouldn't talk this way before May, Winnie."

Winnie had her eyes shut. She made a gesture away with her hands. "Go out, May."

May moved into a shadow by the door, but she did not go out.

"I can't bear being sick. It m-m-makes me so old. Papa Farley—that time Papa Farley—that woman. They had a child, M-m-mother told me. Oh, do you suppose Laurence will do like that?"

"Like what?" Alice's voice was sharp—almost threatening—with distrust.

Winnie kept her eyes shut and wrung her hands. "I thought you knew all about it, Alice."

"About what?"

"Don't act as though you couldn't forgive me! That woman out West—and—and your father started to get a divorce and gave it up. I'm so afraid Laurence won't love me any more!"

Alice knew that her parents had had some trouble. It was the year she was away at school. She had heard fragments—allusions. Now she felt strange. She wanted to hear more but could not—not from Winnie's lips. Alice's coarsely fine face burnt bronze with shame. Her sad eyes of thick brown searched Winnie's evasive features distrustfully. "You mustn't talk about this, Winnie," Alice said. "In the first place it has nothing to do with Laurence. You know as well as I do that Laurence cares for nobody but you and never will. I don't believe he feels hard toward you because you want to see your mother."

"Now you're angry with me?"

"I'm not. I'm going upstairs to wash and brush. You cut out this morbid nonsense, Winnie." Alice smiled a hard, kind, dismissing smile, and turned away, walking briskly out with her firm, awkward stride.

May edged out of the shadow and came nearer her mother. It was half dark in the room. Winnie sniffed, oblivious to May. May came and stood very near. She reached over and passed a hesitant hand along the arm of her mother's chair.

Winnie started. May drew back and stood teetering on one foot, her face alternately dark and smiling. "Oh, May, I t-told you to go out."

May hung her head. A sort of shiver like the shimmer of water passed over her pale, uneasy face. She wanted to go toward her mother. Wanted almost unendurably to go. But something in her mother held her off. May was in torment between the two impulses which possessed her equally.

Winnie wiped her eyes. "Come here," she said at

last. May went forward, smiling, trembling, half released. "You love me, May?"

May could not speak. She choked with affirmation. Her face was in Winnie's warm neck. May lost herself in the warm throat and the soft hair. If she did not have to see her mother's eyes it was well. May had a terror of eyes. They made her know things about herself which she could not bear. Sharp looks splintered her consciousness.

Winnie, overcoming a shudder, admitted the caress. "You'll always love Mother, won't you?"

*   *   *

After the evening meal Mr. Farley took a newspaper into the living-room. There he sat by the lamp with the green shade. Through the still room the light, concentrated under the lamp shade, rushed to the carpet. On the way it spread, glistening, over the oak table, and brightened one-half of Mr. Farley's face. The newspaper in his hands was glassy with light. The print looked gray.

The rain that made the air sharp had not yet fallen and the dim curtains against the open windows shook now and then as with sudden palpitant breaths.

Alice walked about the room nervously. Several times she went to the window and glanced out. When she pulled the curtain back her father's newspaper flapped against his hand, but he showed no impatience.

Alice came and stood before his chair. "Come go for a walk with me!"

"Walk?" He looked up at her. He was vaguely patient and smiling a little. "Isn't it raining?"

"No. Come along." Alice took his arm. He folded his paper carefully and placed it on the table. Then, stiff and heavy in his movements, he got up.

Alice dragged him into the hall and he took his hat down. "You ought to have something over your head," he said to her.

"Rubbish! It's summer. Come on."

Alice flung the front door wide. The wind took their breaths for a second. He stumbled a little as he followed her down the steps and into the empty street. Overhead the moon, a lurid yellow, scudded between transparent black clouds.

"It's too stormy to walk. We mustn't go far or the rain will catch us."

"It won't yet awhile. I had to get out of that house." Alice linked her arm in his. She could feel his discomfort in her talk as though it came through her sleeve against him.

"I'm sorry to hear you talk about your home like that, Alice." Mr. Farley sounded hurt.

"Who wouldn't! I loathe Mamma—that's all."

Mr. Farley's arm quivered where it brushed Alice's shoulder. "You're unjust to her. She's done the best she can for you."

"Has she! Well, my God, she couldn't have done worse."

"I don't think you're just to her."

They walked on. Alice's heavy skirt beat her ankles

above her stout shoes. Mr. Farley's coat-tails flapped. Paper rustled in the gutter.

"You make me sick about being just to Mamma," Alice said almost tenderly. "Whom was she ever just to? What about being just to yourself?"

"We can't ask too much for ourselves in this life," Mr. Farley said soberly.

"Bosh! I wish to Heaven you had left her that time when you wanted to!"

Mr. Farley was shocked. Alice had never spoken to him like this. His arm quivered more than ever. Unable to reply to her for the moment, he was a dung-beetle, rolling his astonishment over and over and making it ready for speech.

"I hardly know how to answer you, Alice. I don't think there ever was a time when I could have taken any joy which came through a sacrifice of other people's happiness. I——" He was confused by his own words. He stopped talking suddenly. Alice could feel that his body was rigid against hers. He could not forgive her.

"Not even when you loved that Mrs. Wilson, eh?" She remembered the name all at once, having heard it long ago.

Mr. Farley stopped, still. He put his hand to his forehead. His other arm fell away from Alice. It took him an instant to answer her. She tapped her foot on the pavement. The wind whizzed in their ears.

"Alice, I—you are referring to things too personal to—I ought to resent it."

"Resent it. I'd be glad to see you resent something."
She wanted him to strike fire against her mother's dull-
ness.

He could not bear her smile.

"Your mother is a good woman——"

"I suppose she is. God save us from good women!"

Mr. Farley walked on slowly. He walked like an old
man. It made him feel tired when he thought that any-
one questioned the nobility and excellence of his resolution.

"When you have had more experience of life, Alice,
you will see how easily we err, and how it's always better to accept the weight of old burdens rather than
assume new ones."

"I'm not likely to be offered new ones."

"What do you mean?"

"What I say. Ugly old maid at twenty-nine. My
life will go on like this forever and ever."

Mr. Farley was ashamed with Alice because she told
the truth about herself. It hurt him to face her ugliness and not be allowed to lie to her.

"That's morbid talk," he said, walking more slowly
and rubbing his forehead again.

"Bosh! I'm not morbid. My life ends where it began—that's all. You're the one who makes me sick.
Why don't you kick out of this? Why don't you find
somebody with some self-respect who means something
to you, and go off and be happy? Some people may
admire you for all this giving up your soul and allowing it to be spit on, but I don't." Her heart was hard
against him. It relieved her to push her father from

her out into life. It helped her to make him live in
her stead.

Large round raindrops pressed their foreheads softly
like rounded lips. The rain falling through the chill
air was warm.

"I hardly think it has been any sacrifice of my self-
respect for me to do my duty toward your mother,"
he answered resentfully.

They walked on quickly, a little apart. Alice was
silent with irritation. She tried to fill her soul with
the calm of disgust but she was feverish against his
inertia. Mr. Farley felt himself misunderstood.

*　　*　　*

Alice had been reading in bed. It was late at night.
The room was very still. She heard Mrs. Farley's tired
step on the back stair coming up from the kitchen.

"Mamma!" Alice called in a sharp, subdued voice.

Mrs. Farley ambled slowly forward and leaned
against the portal. She squinted at Alice wearily.
"Well?"

"Come in."

"I want to go to bed early. I've had so many things
to do." She entered the room uncertainly and sat on
the edge of a chair. Her tired hands twitched a little
in her slack lap. Her hair was untidy. Sweat glistened on her gray upper lip above her pale brown
mouth. When she turned her head Alice saw the thick
white down on her cheek. Her glasses were on her
nose and behind them her blank eyes regarded her

daughter stealthily. "You don't seem to be well, Alice. I've noticed how fidgety you've been getting in this heat."

"I wish it were only the heat." Alice sat up and hugged her knees with her big bare arms. Her nightgown was loose. It showed her heavy neck and the swell of her large breast. Her hair had slipped down and hung in moist dull locks about her hard intent face. "Do you think this operation Winnie has to go through with is serious?"

Mrs. Farley rocked herself a little. Her heel tapped the carpet restlessly. "I don't know. How can you tell?"

"At any rate her parents can afford to give her the best care."

"Yes, but that's the worst of it! The worst of it. Laurence can't bear to have her take things from them." Mrs. Farley spoke in a worn flat voice and rocked herself again.

"How absurd!"

"Oh, he'll have to let them help. There's nothing else to do."

"I suppose that's why Winnie's always in hysterics lately?"

"Is she?"

"My God, Mamma! Take a little interest in something."

Tears of protest rose in Mrs. Farley's eyes. Her mouth shook. She made an effort to rise, then sank back. "No, I take no interest in anything but work,"

she said bitterly. "Keeping house for you and your
father——"

"Why do you do it, then? My God, you could have
stopped ten years ago." Seeing her mother's eyes fill
with tears, Alice's own dry eyes felt a sudden coolness. "Whom do you do it for? Laurence and I are
old enough to look out for ourselves!"

Mrs. Farley's shoulders drooped and shivered. She
wagged her head on her lean neck in helpless protest
and reproach. Her body rocked. "I suppose your
father don't need me," she said scornfully, crudely
wiping the sweat from her face with her hand. She
looked like a blind woman, hearing Alice from a long
way off.

"Of course he doesn't need you! You ought to have
found that out the time he tried to get a divorce from
you!" Alice, mysteriously urged to cruelty, bore down
upon her mother. Alice's eyes glittered inscrutably.

Mrs. Farley could not bear them. She stood at last,
tottering a little. Her breath came quickly and rasp-
ingly. "Hush, I tell you! Hush! You've brought this
up before. There's something cruel in you makes you
want to go over and over things that are done with!"

"I suppose you think I'm an interfering old maid?"

"I don't know what you are."

"And you don't want to know." Alice sounded
amused. It was an unpleasant sound.

Mrs. Farley, gazing very deliberately at the carpet, blew her nose. "I've never discussed my relation
to your father with his children and I'm not going to

now. I've sacrificed myself for what I thought best
and it's nobody's business but my own."

"Sacrificed!" echoed Alice contemptuously.

"I won't listen to you and that's all there is to it.
I never expected gratitude so I'm not disappointed."
Mrs. Farley, not looking back, dragged into the hall.

Alice lay still an instant, her expression one of relentless retrospect. Her eyes were enigmatic but her
mouth was twisted with disgust and her nostrils were
wide and tense. She reached above her head and turned
out the light.

The curtain flapped. Staccato fingers of rain tapped
on the pane.

In the room it was dark. The narrow dark. The
walls of the room drew near. She felt herself pressed
between them.

Alice tossed from side to side. When she lay quiet
finally the darkness receded from her, touched her lids
softly in passing.

Death! Oh, my God, I want life!

She sat up in bed holding her heavy breasts. Father!
A great body unmotivated. Alice's hot will sought for
a world to impregnate. Wish-washy mother who had
given birth meaninglessly.

Horace Ridge. She grew cool with despair—de-
sireless.

The hot sheets turned cool. Far away the beat of
rain on the window. Under the lifted sash the rain-wet
wind swept through the room, frozen pain, threads of
frozen wonder embroidering the hot dark. Wet wind

beat the soggy awnings against the glass. A dank smell came in.

*   *   *

It was a cold August morning. The pale sky was filled with a dim still light. In the dining-room the yellow shades, half lowered, strained the gloomy radiance through them and made it a heavy orange. The tablecloth, splattered with coffee stains like old blood, was overcast with trembling reflections of yellow. The morning meal was over. The empty plates were scattered about smeared with hardened egg. The half of a muffin was mashed on the dingy carpet.

Mr. Farley, a little away from the table, sat reading his paper. Mrs. Farley was collecting the débris of breakfast. Her feeble hands moved among the dishes with shaken determination.

"Was your egg fried enough?" she asked.

"Yes, yes. Very nice." Mr. Farley glanced up and gave his wife a sightless smile. Troubled by what Alice had said to him, he was uncomfortable when Mrs. Farley spoke. He began to fold his paper.

What he was finished with, he pushed out of his mind into darkness. Alice had dragged his memories, and now the past came up to him like a corpse floating. Helen out West. She might come East next month. He hoped not. His son. Place where he sent money. He paid to be allowed to stop thinking about it.

"I'm worried about Winnie. I thought her reconciliation with her parents would improve her frame of mind, but now she seems more nervous and unhappy than ever. The thought of that operation preys on her mind."

"Well—I think she ought to go out into the country for a rest before there's any more talk of operation."

"She thinks Laurence will never be able to forgive her if she goes off with her mother and father."

"Oh, now I think that's too bad. She mustn't think things like that about Laurence." Mr. Farley talked kindly with a sort of clerical remoteness. His lips smiled wearily. His head was bent. He stood up.

Mrs. Farley picked up her pile of dishes; put the dishes between herself and life. The talk with Alice the night before had made Mrs. Farley feel furtive.

"Don't work too hard." Mr. Farley walked out.

Mrs. Farley saw May outside in the hall. "Come here, May. See if you can help me take the plates to the kitchen."

May came in, glad to be called. Her grandmother did not look at her. She picked up a plate with a cup on it. She walked into the kitchen, taking careful steps, the rim of the plate, held with both hands, pressed so tightly against her breast that it cut. The cup jiggled rhythmically, bumping time to May's steps. May's mouth hung open. Her face was bewildered with anxiety. Her breath came fast. With immense relief she reached the sink and, leaning over, slipped the plate into it.

Mrs. Farley had to talk to some one. She wanted to push the trifles forward in her life and crowd back the darkness, filling it with bright hard things, baubles, grocerymen, and dishes; so she asked May, "Has our groceryman gone by here this morning? He promised to call and exchange that condensed milk for evaporated milk."

"No'm," May said.

Mrs. Farley, frowning, her brows twitching, looked at May. Mrs. Farley could not see the little girl without feeling an irritable prompting to command her. "Go wash your face and see if your mother is awake. If she isn't, don't rouse her. Don't let Bobby see you or he'll begin to clamor to get out of bed."

May ran dutifully out.

"Don't clatter up the steps!" Mrs. Farley called sharply.

May walked very softly up the creaking stairs.

Mrs. Farley had the soiled clothes to count. She left the dishes to soak and went into the dining-room again with the big bundle tied in a sheet.

"One, two, three, four." She untied the sheet and began to count. She could not count fast enough. She crammed her mind with numbers. It was like trying to fill a slack sack to cover something hidden at the bottom.

"Shirts. Socks."

Not darned. Must darn today. Alice's stockings. Alice is a hard, selfish girl.

"Tablecloths. Two—two"—murmuring—"what did I say?"

Sacrifice. We must all make sacrifices. The home.

"One, two."

Her heart smoldered damply in its resignation. She squeezed love out of her heart.

Those awful days! Ten years older. People one did not know seemed to seek one accusingly in the street.

Furtively, she recalled the birth of her son, remembrance of a strength that had somehow become weariness. Winnie.

In the dark doorway Winnie appeared in a muslin dress. She was smiling, a little wan. Her hair was dressed high. She looked plaintive yet determined.

"I won't be sick and lie around," she said. "I'm going to help you work."

"You're going to do nothing of the sort! You sit right down here and I'll give you your breakfast at once. Did that child wake you up after all?"

"No. I was awake."

"Well, sit down."

"Oh, Mamma Farley, I want to fix my own egg." Winnie, protesting without conviction, allowed herself to be pressed into a chair.

"Where did you leave Bobby?"

"He's still asleep."

"Well, you had no business to get up."

Winnie gazed up with sweet greedy eyes. "I don't dare be sick any more. Sick people are horrid. Nobody loves them." Winnie's mouth was patient, quivering, below her lifted eyes.

"Yes. Nobody loves them." Mrs. Farley joked laboriously.

"You dear!" Winnie reached out and grasped Mrs. Farley's hand. Winnie's eyes, like brown bees, crept

with their glance into the vague combative eyes before them. Thinking of yesterday's talk, Winnie's gaze
pierced the rough-dried pongee blouse and the sagging
black skirt, and saw the small high-shouldered form
beneath. Winnie's looks invited to pain as to a bath
of wine enjoyed with closed eyes.

Mrs. Farley's eyes filled with tears. Ugly and old,
before Winnie's pity Mrs. Farley was a woman beaten
back by a lover. She put forth a smile that was like
a weak and gentle hand caressing an enemy. "Bless
you, dear. You sit still while I get your breakfast."

She walked out quickly.

* * *

When Laurence came home to dinner Winnie, still
dressed in her best, was alone in the living-room.

"Hello! You've assumed a new rôle," he said from
the doorway.

She could see that finding her there made him uncomfortable. She smiled at him with a kind of happy pain.

He came forward. He was kind and distant. His
lips brushed her hair.

She gazed up at him. Her eyes, with crushed back
lids and lifted lashes, melted open for his.

"I don't want to be sick, Laurie. I've got to go
away with Mother. You won't hate me for going away
with her? I do need a change so!"

He stood before her with a kind of mocking fatigue,
but she saw that he was sunk deep in himself. She
wanted to drag him up.

He shook his head. "I don't know what to say to you lately."

She reached up and laced him with her arms. "Am I so unreasonable? Oh, Laurie, I don't want to die."

He seated himself helplessly on the arm of her chair. "Why think about something so improbable as dying?"

"But I might. I want you to care," she whispered.

"Don't you think I care?" His voice had a grating note as he tried to be light.

"Of course—yes—I guess so. But it's so awful to think about."

"Then don't think of it."

"I can't help it."

Death. The word had not been alive to her until this moment. Suddenly she heard it about her, whispering like wings. She floated beyond Laurence, beyond the room.

With a quick intake of breath she shut out terror grown too delicious.

"Then you will let me go away with Mother? You won't stop loving me, Laurie?"

"I'll shake you for talking nonsense," he said, getting up.

She hated him for escaping her, but her mind was made up and the next day when her mother called the morning of departure was set.

* * *

Settling her pince-nez on her flat nose before her fixed and despairing eyes, Mrs. Price pressed Winnie's

face to her flat black bosom. "I'm so glad, dear. It
was so foolish of my little girl to hold out against
having her parents do anything for her. Your father
is so good, Winnie. There is nothing I can ask for you
that he isn't willing to give. You mustn't deprive him
of that pleasure."

Winnie thought of Laurie and was stiff in her
mother's embrace, yet at that moment could not have
said which of them was most irritating.

Mrs. Price always avoided Laurence's name.

When Mrs. Price had gone Winnie lay in her room
on the couch, excited and oppressed. She said death
to herself, and the word echoed inside her like a cry
down a long hall. Then the echo was lost in the deeps
of darkness. But it continued to quiver below the surface of her life.

Winnie thought of being sick. She was harsh with
a knowledge of herself. She would not be sick. Closing her eyes she imagined her mouth. With a kind of
horror of its own act, it pressed Laurence's. She
woke up.

The noonday sun outside was pale with rain. Winnie heard footsteps in the still noon street. Death.
The dancing word fluttered ahead of the hurrying feet.

Winnie moved fretfully on the couch. She saw
Death as the face of an insistent stranger thrust into
her own. Stupid thing which she did not know. She
pushed it aside feebly, feeling for what had meaning
to her—Laurence, Bobby, Mrs. Price.

All at once she realized that Laurence had come home
for something and was in the room. He rummaged at

his desk. He was subdued in his movements, trying
not to rouse her. She watched him between half-closed
lids. He was familiar to her. The very crooked set
of his thick neck in his broad shoulders was food to
her. Hungrily she opened her eyes wider and lifted
herself to her elbow.

"What's the matter, Laurie?" Her whisper, sharp
and sweet, pierced the somber stillness of the room
where the shades had been drawn for her to rest.

"Hellò! I came to get a note book. Did I wake
you?" He had started at the sound of his name, but
as he faced her he held himself contained in his sharp
cold smile.

"I don't care. I've been having horrid dreams,
Laurie."

"That's a silly thing to do."

"Don't make fun of me. Come sit by me a minute."

"I haven't much time, dear." He came and sat on
the edge of the couch. "Don't you want the shades
up? It's so gloomy."

"I want you first. See how cold my hands are!"

She gave him her hands. He took them as though
he did not know what to do with them. His eyes were
still full of the brightness of the street and he could
not see her plainly.

"I want you to love me. Oh, Laurie, you do love
me!" She groped up his arms, his cheek, until she
had found his mouth. She covered it up with her hand.
She did not want it to speak against her. When he
tried to talk she pulled him down until his eyes pressed
her breast. She drew him deeper into the warm covers

on the tumbled couch. She was cold. Her hands said
that he must warm her. Memories of pain were silver
veins in her body. Twisting herself on the couch to
bring him nearer, she wrenched her arm, sharp pang
of happiness.

"Love me!" she entreated. Her mouth clung against
his. She could feel the force of his quickening heart
beats as though they were her own. The muscles in
his arm twitched under the rough-napped cloth of the
sleeve which brushed her cheek. Her nostrils dilated
against his arm. The smell of his body was bitter. She
wanted to drink in the vividness of his strong live
flesh that resisted her.

Around the dimmed squares of the yellow shades,
light, entering, made shining borders. Noises drifted
in the light under the bright edges of the yellow shades.
Hammering from the house on the corner reverberated
through the room.

"Winnie! I can't—you mustn't. You're not well
enough. You mustn't excite yourself like this!"

She felt him passive in his resistance. Reluctantly
her arms slipped away. Her resentful eyes shone at
him from the gloom with a small and pointed light.

He leaned away from her, patting her hair as he
came gradually to his feet. He did not want to see her
because she made him feel guilty toward himself. Then
he was obliged to look. When he smiled at her he kept
her outside his eyes. He seemed relieved in spite of
himself.

"Poor little sick girl," he said as to a child. "I'm

glad you're going away with your mother. We'll give you a nice rest and have you all fixed up."

"You don't love me!" she said, looking at him stormily.

"Please, Winnie. Things are hard enough." His face was drawn with the effort of his continued smile.

"You don't." She turned over and closed her eyes.

"Don't be absurd." He joked uncomfortably.

But she would not look at him.

He walked out on tiptoe as though he thought her asleep.

When she knew he was gone she began to cry, and, keeping her eyes closed, moved her head from side to side and struck into the pillows with her fist.

* * *

Laurence did not go home to dinner, but remained working at the laboratory until after midnight. As he walked home the city streets, washed thinly with light, were yet thronged. His mind was sharply intent on itself. It was like the keel of a ship, parting the swarming life before it.

But as he drew nearer the place where Winnie was his heart strained. He felt suffocated. There were women standing in doorways. Their shadows wove the darkness together and drew it tight about his heart. He hated his work but the doing of it gave him relief, for it could not enter him.

The glow from a street lamp fell on his own house —purple-red walls that held Winnie. The big gilt figures on the transom above the door glistened on the glass that gave back a blank reflection of the light. He put in his latch key. The door, swinging away from nim, seemed drawn inward with the pull of the darkness.

It shut ponderously behind him. He hesitated a moment, resisting some unknown inevitability. It was very still in the dark.

Only the stairs were half revealed by the pallor of the light that came in high up from the street.

He walked up softly and opened the bedroom door. He could hear a breath like the respiration of shadow. He knew it was Bobby.

Then somehow he realized that Winnie was awake and holding herself apart from the dark.

He did not speak. She did not speak. He sat down and began to take off his shoes.

As he laid the shoes away from him he was aware of her awareness as though she were seeing him stoop forward in the dark. He had a sense of his own motion as a pale line etched across a thick surface. When he unbuckled his belt and began to draw his trousers over his feet he felt the sharp sweep of his moving arms tearing the quiescence of the room.

He stood up naked. His cold toes gripped the hot nap of the roughened carpet. He pulled on his pajamas and the white cloth, as it was drawn up his legs, was cool white fire, that burnt upward from his bare feet.

The room seemed a final blackness into which the dark of the night outside had flowed and gathered as in a pool. Still feeling himself burning white in the cool cloth, Laurence walked to the side of the bed and looked down to see if Winnie were asleep.

Very faintly he saw the rigid line of her body, but through her nightdress he perceived her tense, like a protest. He could not see her eyes but he shivered with the feeling that they were very wide open and sightless. The darkness was against her eyes, holding her rigid upon the white sheet in the dark bed.

"Laurie!"

"I thought you were asleep." He did not know why he lied.

She did not answer at once and he stood waiting. "Laurie!"

He felt suddenly feverish in his cold clothes.

She reached out and touched him. The feel of her hand flowed along his hand and up the veins of his arm. He felt as though her hand had been laid upon his heart. His heart beat quickly. He denied his heart. He was passive. He stood apart from himself. He was unrelated to Winnie, sick and tense in the bed.

"Laurie!" she whispered again. She drew him down beside her.

"You are sick, Winnie," he said. Sure of himself, he did not resist her.

She reached up, groping to cover his mouth. It made her angry when he told her she was sick. She did not want him to build up words between them. She tried to draw him into herself, into the formlessness of contact.

"Oh, I can't sleep, Laurie! I want you to love me."

"I do love you, Winnie. If I seem not to love you it is because you are sick."

"I'm not sick! I won't be sick. You don't love me!"

"I do!"

"Please love me! I'll die if you don't love me, Laurie!"

He resisted her.

She drew his hand to her and placed it like a cup over the swell of her breast.

He trembled. "Winnie, my darling, we mustn't——"

"Laurie, I'll go mad!"

"Why, Winnie? I love you, Winnie."

But he did not love her. She seemed to him like a sickness. They were both sick with her.

"Kiss me again."

He kissed her. His palm tingled with the strangeness of her breast.

"I can't let you go 'way from me, Laurie!"

"I don't want to."

She held him. Suddenly she was no longer strange. His hand read the strangeness of her with the relief of familiarity. She burned him with wonder.

Winnie felt him yield and was glad, but her triumph congealed in agony. She fell away from him. She was cold. She was still. The throbbing of her body came to her like an echo which she could scarcely hear. She had forgotten the meaning of it. Who was this man? She was afraid.

She waited for him to leave her.

* * *

Laurence was tired with the feeling of Winnie that flowed through his body. She was in his veins degrading him with possession.

If she should have a child. He would not think of it. He walked over to the couch and climbed upon it. He would not think. Driving his thoughts from him, as he lay down, he felt the flap of the window shade and the respiration of Bobby rattling in his empty mind.

He tossed. His body was hot. The sheet he pulled over him made him shiver. Then he grew cold and longed for the heat to cover him up. He felt naked. He wanted to lie drowned in heat, miles thick in darkness.

*   *   *

Winnie awoke. It was morning. The room was cool and bright. Sunshine made the curtains glow. Patches of light shuddered delicately here and there on the carpet. A spear of sunshine shattered itself on the looking-glass.

Laurence slept on the couch with one arm tossed up and his head thrown back. His mouth was open. His face in sleep seemed stupid with pain. Bobby slept, too, stirring and murmuring a little. Winnie found something oppressive in the sight of people yet asleep like this in the full blaze of the sun.

Winnie's mind was clear and calm with the ease that came of sleep, but in the center of her being there was a dark spot of indecipherable vividness.

Last night. A dark spot of terror. Laurence had

been frightened by what they had done. She wanted him to be frightened.

Death. If she had a child she would suffer—not he. White and holy, she felt herself a beautiful stillness in the turmoil of Laurence's cowardice.

She could not part with this fear. If she had a child Death was her hand from which he could not escape.

*   *   *

Midnight. The street lamps shone into the bedroom, making bright shadows of the drawn shades. The bureau, the bed, bits of furniture here and there, darker than the darkness, reflected the light heavily.

Laurence stood outside the door in the hall. He was trembling, afraid of his own room. He had stayed away all day because he could not see Winnie, because he hoped that when he reached home she would be asleep.

It was quiet. He opened the door and stepped inside. The sudden draught lifted the shades ponderously and let them drop again.

Fresh, clean wind from the quiet midnight street surged into the room. Light floated in under the lifted shades. It seemed as if the wind, cold and shining, were washing away the darkness.

Winnie was awake again. Laurence stood still.

He waited a long time. He felt shaken. If I take her again she will die.

He did not believe it. He went toward her with a

nausea of relief. "Die" was the word of a song. It was the strange music of passion that said die.

He waited by the bed. He wanted her to tell him to go away. He could feel her still and looking at him.

When he knelt by the bed and reached his arms around her he wanted her to evade him.

"Winnie?" She trembled when he touched her. He wanted her to speak. But she was quiet.

She let him kiss her mouth.

Death. His understanding could not hold the vagueness of the strange escaping word. He felt her thinning from his grasp. His veins swelled with death.

Then he became the death-giver, glad, in spite of himself, of the drunkenness of moving with the unseen. Through the banality of sex which oppressed him, there pushed the will of an exalted and passionate horror.

He took her. They were dead.

*   *   *

Winnie lay face downward and sobbed. There was no triumph in her now. She felt herself as if already large with child, heavy and helpless. Through the darkness of her closed lids she could see, as if before her, Laurence's coarse and handsome head, his eyes turned toward her with their strained gaze, and the odd set of his neck that kept his face always a little to one side. She knew now how much she hated him.

*   *   *

Laurence, walking along the deserted streets, was

relieved to find the long vistas ending in darkness. The
night rose high and expressionless before him. Beyond the dim lights, the violet-blue horizon was a clear
quiet stretch like a lake of glass covered with flowering
stars.

His pain was choked in him, suffocated by the quiet.

His mind was sick yet with Winnie's sickness, but
the pain of her no longer belonged to him. He wondered if she would have a child, if he had killed her.
But the agony of his conjecture related to something
already finished. She had made him love her against
them both. He did not want love like that. It could
never be otherwise. They were separated from each
other by their own bodies.

PART II

A S Mr. Farley walked home from business he had a
troubled look. When he came into his own street
he scarcely seemed aware of his whereabouts. For several days he had been restless and ill at ease with himself. His resentment toward Alice was blunted and dis-
persed by his determination to think well of the world.
He needed this charity to think well of himself. What
disturbed and depressed him most was her forcible sug-
gestion of incompleteness in things which he had looked
upon as finished.

He went up the steps. There was a Kansas City
newspaper in the box. It hurt him to take it out and
put it in his pocket.

When he opened the front door and stepped into
the empty hall, the first look of the place pained him
with its harsh familiarity; but, when he had laid his
hat down, he passed on into the living-room and seated
himself in one of the old tapestry-covered chairs, and
his antagonism and desire to exist in separateness
melted in the faintly bitter sense of inevitability which
he experienced. The old house with the low ceilings
and broad stone mantelpieces and the walls hung in
stained, dark figured papers (just as he had bought it
with the first savings of his married life) represented

100

the known, asserting him through his identity with it.

He leaned forward, closing his eyes and pinching his lids together between his thumbs and forefingers.

Mrs. Farley had heard him come. She could not keep away. When she entered the room, however, she pretended to be surprised.

"I—oh, I didn't hear you! I came for a dust cloth. Winnie has gone out in the Price's carriage to do some shopping." Mrs. Farley scattered her words before her as a cuttlefish throws out its vaguely disguising substance.

Mr. Farley lifted his head with a heavy, patient smile, but she would not look at him.

"Well, well. I thought that dust cloth was here." She fumbled among the chairs. She was very matter-of-fact and intent. She saw that he was depressed and it made her uneasy.

Mr. Farley could see her profile: her lined, withered lips, her dry, finely wrinkled skin which was a thin film of disguise over her melting flesh. The expression of nervous good humor in her evasive eyes was like a gauze scarf laid over a spectacle of horror.

The two people, afraid of their fear of each other, were like alien creatures haltered with one chain.

"Can I help you?" Mr. Farley asked.

"No. No. Alice hasn't come home, has she?"

"As far as I know, she hasn't. Shall I send her to you when she comes?"

"No. That's all right! That's all right!"

Mrs. Farley hurried out. She went into the dining-room. A last streak of sunshine filtered through the

clouds and came over the back yard into the room.
There were some tumblers in a tray on the sideboard
that caught the specks of light that were like bubbles
of fire in the colorless glass. Each day the sun touched
the same spots with the same light. There was assurance and finality in the undeviating rays of the tired
sun. Mrs. Farley felt quiet among the chairs and
tables. She saw some lint on the ragged sun-washed
carpet, and stooped to pick it off. She craved intimacy with the still things her touch could dominate.
They enlarged her. And she was afraid of those who
would speak some terrible word of love or money to
destroy their permanence.

When she went to the sideboard and opened the
drawer in which the tablecloths were kept, her furtive
thoughts slipped between the linen, and, as her hands
moved over it, the cool glazed feel of the starched fabric
was a denial of change and heat.

In the living-room, Mr. Farley leaned back in his
chair again, his eyes half closed. In his low chair his
gaze was on a level with the polished top of the table,
glazed silverish with the dimming light. The arms of
the imitation mahogany rocker were as bright and
enigmatic as glass. Some pictures on the wall were indecipherable beneath streaked reflections.

An old painting of Lake Lucerne hung over the mantel shelf. The pigment was faded and the canvas was
seamed with fine, irregular cracks. When Mr. Farley
glanced upward at this picture he experienced a voluptuous sense of futility. He stared at it a long time.

But the spell of inertia did not last. He became

uneasy again. He was afraid his wife might come back,
so he walked across the hall to the disorderly little room
that was called his "study."

There were a desk, and a leather lounge with pro-
truding springs, and, on the walls, two or three old
advertising calendars decorated with hunting scenes or
full-color pictures of setter dogs.

Mr. Farley sat down before the littered desk and
began his letter, "Dear Helen."

He wrote to her about his regard for her and their
mutual sense of responsibility toward their son, and
he wanted to say something else. But when he attempted to recall more intimate phrases it revived his
sense of sin. He felt embarrassed and gave it up.

* * *

It was seven o'clock in the evening. The sun had
gone. The sky at the zenith was pale, but along the
horizon the foam-white clouds glowed with pink. From
the city light had receded like a tide and rows of housetops on the length of the sky were like objects left there
by a departing sea. They were separate and waited.

As darkness gathered, it gathered first in the house
fronts like an added heaviness. Above the houses the
sky floated—higher, paler. The sky dilated and
soared.

Then the shining pallor grew dim. The sky sent itself down in grayness to the dark streets where the lamp
lights floated in the dust as in clouds of ash. The

house fronts, flaked with light, disintegrated in the general vagueness.

Horace Ridge was ready to depart. On his last night before sailing he had sent for Alice to help him finish some work. She passed out of the twilight into the tiled corridor of the building in which he lived. The marble walls wavered in light. Lights, clustered above the wainscot, stabbed her eyes. A sleepy hallboy in a tan uniform vacantly watched her approach.

She ignored the elevators and walked up the one flight of stairs and along the brown velvet carpet to the door she wanted. When she rang the small bell under the brass plate she heard the tinkle in the depths of her being, sharp, like a light moving under deep water. So keen was her perception of his coming that she was not conscious of separate incidents—footsteps, the sigh of the opening door. But in one act he was there in the place where she had expected him.

He held a hand over his eyes that were guarded with a green shade.

"Miss Alice. I'm merciless these days. Must get something done while the doing of it is in me." He smiled with his mouth, his eyes mysterious out of sight.

"You're merciless to yourself. We all know that," Alice said.

He walked after her into the library. Without seeing him, she was aware of the uncertainty of his tired steps. She was ashamed of her deep consciousness of his hesitation, knowing that he tried to conceal his half gestures from her.

He sat down rather heavily and she stood in the center of the book-lined room, unpinning her hat.

"I would like to have taken you for a lark on my last night instead of setting you to work. You'll be glad to forget about me." His mouth still smiled and his big hand moved up to his eyes under the shade.

Alice did not answer. Then she said, "Are you sure you feel well enough to work?" She had the brusque presumptuous manner which she knew he tolerated.

"The old dog has a lot of fight in him yet. You mustn't draw too many conclusions from appearances."

The big room with the high shelves was gloomy in candle light.

"These esthetic shadows will spoil your eyes. You'd better get that student lamp down," he said.

Alice walked briskly to a stand in the corner and took down the light. She carried it over to his table.

"You'd better move. It shines there." It hurt her to tell him what to do.

"I'll sit with my back to it."

Alice pushed a heap of books aside and arranged the green cord attachment over the crowded table.

Blindness. Better after all. He can't see me, she thought bitterly.

She sat down with her writing pad in her lap.

He rubbed his forehead wearily. His shoulders sagged, big beneath his loose coat. There was passive strength in his consciousness of defeat. She was aware of it.

The room closed them like a coffin. Their life was their own. It did not flow in from the street.

Beyond the window the square was sprinkled with lights. The thick-leafed trees were clouds of darkness, but here and there separate leaves up against the lamps glistened like wet metal.

He sighed. "I'm trying to line up my vocabulary in battle order, Miss Alice."

"I'm ready. Go ahead."

He did not begin at once. She watched his bowed head—thick, gray-sprinkled brown hair. There was beard on his cheek.

Suddenly she had a horror of herself creeping upon his thoughts through his weakness. She shuddered, shifting her book.

Dark. Flesh, aware of the world, slipping away. Flesh touched by the world without.

"As regards the international polity of the——"

She interrupted. "Say that again, Mr. Ridge." He had dictated several sentences and she had not heard him.

"Since the——" She began to write. The wind fluttered the paper on her knee. Her hands with big knuckles moved decisively over the sheet.

* * *

"I'm wearing you out?"

"Bother! You're not!"

He liked her positiveness. "A half a paragraph or so and I will have reached the end of my tether."

"Go ahead."

When he had finished he leaned back, turning himself

so that he could look at her, and she could tell by his mouth that he was happier.

"I've taxed your patience."

"Haven't any patience," Alice said, making a wry face. She wanted to cry.

She stood up. "I'll have this all typed by tomorrow afternoon. When does the boat sail?"

"Ten tomorrow night."

They were silent. He still smiled, his blunt fingers tapping the arm of his chair, but the corners of his full lips sagged with fatigue under the stiff edges of his mustache and he was pale.

Alice got her hat down from the shelf.

"You need some one to take care of you," she said, trying to sound angry. She was afraid her words hurt him. Her heart beat very fast.

"Young Harrison is going along to keep me from walking overboard in an absent moment."

They were quiet again. Alice could not make up her mind to go out. The trees in the square seemed to have crowded closer against the open windows. The leaves looked like tin in the auras of light. She stared into the street that had grown still.

"Well—if I don't get down to the boat I'll send somebody." She held out her hand.

He stood up. Being so big, he looked more helpless behind his shade. He took her hand and held it in both his.

"God bless you, Miss Alice."

She could not speak.

He saw that she was disturbed. He was kind, a big stout man, smiling. Her throat closed.

"Take a real rest," she ordered in a short, thick, over-casual voice. Their hands dropped apart.

"I'll probably be forced to in spite of myself."

"Well, I'm glad of it." She turned quickly and went toward the door. He followed her and stumbled a little. She tried not to look back at him.

"This has been awfully good of you," he said after her in his slow, kind way.

She could not bear his slow kindness. She did not answer.

"Can't I get a taxicab for you?"

"Couldn't. Feel uncomfortable with such luxuries. You go to bed and rest."

She glanced back once. He stood, huge in his fatigue, with his drooped, gentle mouth, in an attitude as if he did not know what to do with his hands.

"Good-bye."

She bit her lips. "Good-bye."

The door closed. She was in the corridor stupid with light. On the stairs she met the hallboy, who stood aside. He had a vacant gaze as if the empty brilliance of the hall had dizzied him.

When she passed into the still street she felt as though she slipped into an inner darkness. She was two and the self that suffered, heavy and dark, sank through an oblivious other and out of knowledge.

I cannot bear it!

She went through the park. There were people on

the benches in the darkness. She walked quickly past them into the bare-swept circles under the lamps.

What shall I do? Lies. I think I'm going mad.

She went on. Her heels clicked on the deserted street. Against the window of a house she passed a lamp with a red shade glowed softly. The new moon over the trees was like a fragment of ice.

What does it come to? Sheep. Wag. Wag tail. Mistress Mary. Far away over the hills. The street. Dark over the hills. Dark. Darkness is one. There are no eyes in the dark.

Horace.

Walking, she pressed her knuckles against her lips and dug her teeth into the flesh. Sweet to feel. Softly her agony flowed through the wound of her teeth.

When she reached home she passed quickly through the dimly lit hallway and so up the long stairs, escaping notice.

The hinges creaked as she opened the door of her dark room. She went in quickly and closed it and rested against the lintel, panting, her head thrown back.

Her mind was fire and ice. She must kill this agony.

A little light floated in from the street through the open window. She could see her bureau with its white cover and the sparkle of toilet instruments on it. She went there and picked up a pair of scissors, plunging the points twice into her flesh with quick stabs.

Feeling numbness and relief, she stood stupidly watching the blood, dark and colorless, gather on her forearm.

Mary had a little lamb. I'm mad. Washed in the
blood of the lamb.

She sank to her knees, then relaxed on the floor in
a half sitting posture, her head thrown back against
the bed, her hat awry, one hand holding the ache of
her bleeding wrist, the glow from the street lamp be-
wildering her eyes.

*   *   *

Mr. Price, gruff and solemn, tried to hasten the departure. "Well, Winifred, you're ready?" His smoky
eyes were everywhere and on no one. He waved the
hand that held his hat.

Winnie had on a new cloak and a pretty little blue
straw turban. . . . Laurie will be angry when he sees
Mother has been buying me clothes.

"Bobby—Bobby, my darling!" She hugged him to
her, trying to wring from him some assurance that she
would be with him when she was gone.

Allowing himself to be kissed, he stirred an instant
and was calm. He was water, broad and profound.
Winnie felt herself sinking into his passive depths.
"Oh, Bobby!"

"You hurts my arm."

She drew away from him and felt part of her still
there, lost in his passive clearness.

"You won't forget Mamma? Mamma Farley will
help you write me letters. You know how you can
print—nice printing with pictures? I'm going to bring

you something beautiful. Grandma Price and I are
going to bring you something—oh, lovely!"

"Yes, my dear. We'll have something nice for a good
little boy who doesn't forget us." Mrs. Price touched
his hair with taut, wistful gestures.

Winnie's cheeks were bright.

Mrs. Price had on a trim black traveling suit of
handsome cloth and a simple but distinguished hat,
very precisely worn.

"Is Laurie upstairs, Mamma Farley?"

Mrs. Farley looked up, abstracted. She dangled in
the general emotion like a puppet suspended over a
torrent, swayed but unmoved. "I think so, dear." She
tried not to see Mrs. Price, so like herself but lifted
up by social confidence.

"I'm going up to see him."

"All right, dear."

"Nine o'clock," Mr. Price said sternly, taking out his
watch and looking at it with an air of reprimand.

"Just a moment, Father."

Winnie ran up the long dingy stairs to the door of
her room. It was open and before she entered she
saw Laurence standing in the confusion of packing
which she had left, and looking at a book.

When she stood beside him he glanced up carefully.
His lips were drawn. She thought he smiled at her as
if she were a stranger.

"Off?"

She was breathing quickly, her eyes shining at him
reproachfully through her fluff of hair under the new
hat.

The gas light to one side made his hair glossy and threw shadows in the hollows of his cheeks.

"Aren't you going to the train, Laurie?"

"Don't you think the family will be happier if I am not there to spoil the rapport of departure?" Smiling, he stared at her with his hard, pained eyes. She had the feeling that he was a long way off. She felt sorry for herself.

"Oh, Laurie, please have some pity for me! Don't be nasty tonight."

"It's pity for you that keeps me here, my dear girl." She could not speak. Death. I may be pregnant. A sharp, small fear bit her breast with its teeth. Because she was hurt inside she despised his ignorance. She wanted to poison his calm with her fear, but the triumph of injury was sweet to her. She held it close.

"You'll be glad now." She was trembling.

"Glad of what, dear girl?"

"That I'm gone."

"Winnie, please? Not tonight." He gazed straight at her. His smiling patience was too bitter. Her pride could not forgive him. Tears of shame and hate rose to her eyes.

"You don't love me any more. I know that."

He would not look at her. Turning over the leaves of the book, his small hand shook. Its whiteness and delicacy irritated her.

"Oh, Laurie, I can't go away angry!" She put her hand on his sleeve. The roughness and realness of his sleeve hurt her hand. She did not want it.

Without looking up, he reached an arm around her.

THE NARROW HOUSE   113

"Have you talked to the doctor, Winnie?" He could not look at her.

"Yes," she whispered, lying. When she lied she blamed him more.

"Are you sure you're all right, Winnie?" He forced out the words very deliberately. They were like stones to his lips.

She hesitated an instant. Then she said, "Yes. Kiss me. Oh, Laurie, it's so awful I—it's so awful I——"

He put the book down and faced her in her embrace. She thought he seemed calm and satisfied as though the doctor had become proxy for his conscience. Winnie's eyes, fiercely soft, stared into his and made him feel furtive and depressed. He kissed her to keep from looking at her.

When their mouths were together his cruelty made her strong. She forgave him. He was a dark thing close to her, smothering her with his breath. His clothed body dissolved in her immediate recognition of his flesh, and she had a sickish sensation as of life stirring in her. Shamelessly kind and unmoved, he had believed this impossible thing.

She moved away from him in spite of herself and with a pang she felt how his hand dropped away in relief that she did not want it. She would not go away.

"You don't love me!"

"Please don't let us torture each other, Winnie. You are going away to get well."

"Suppose I should die, Laurence."

"But you won't die." Again he drew her uncomfortably to him. His head throbbed. He tried to give her what she wanted.

Her shuddering lips moved over his face and he drooped helplessly under them like a beast in the rain. He tried to love her.

She hated him so that she could not bear to have him go away from her. Death. She tried to keep that word in her. It was a child she had conceived to which she refused birth. She wanted to carry death dead in her.

"If anything terrible happens—if I have to be operated on!" Her words stumbled.

"But nothing will happen. You're nervous, Winnie. You're all nervous and sick. This stay in the country will make you over."

"And you'll be glad to see me well again?" She leaned back from him, searching his set, kind face with her tearful eyes.

"Of course, my dear girl. Of course."

"Winnie!" Alice called.

"I'm coming!" Winnie gave him another swift little bitter kiss and slipped from his arms. As she went out she glanced back, smiling and pathetic. He hurt her and she wanted to remind him how pretty she was. She was small and light with dread.

His being composed itself in darkness and peace, but his composure was an ache, blank and broad.

*   *   *

Above the housetops huge masses of cloud, smutted like torrents of gray-white snow, moved steadily, surf of a gigantic tide sweeping the purplish-blue stillness of the far vacant sky. It was noonday.

Alice passed briskly up the steps and opened the dusty front door.

"Mamma?"

Mrs. Farley was in the dusk-shrouded living-room behind drawn shades. She did not answer. When she heard Alice's heavy footsteps she shivered.

Alice came to the living-room door and looked in. Her mother squinted at her bewilderedly, then glanced away.

"You still here, are you? I've been down and finished up the business Mr. Ridge left me to do."

Mrs. Farley rose wearily, as if driven. Her knees were slack under her trailing skirt. Her posture sagged. "I should have started the children's lunch," she said.

"I'll start the children's lunch, but it is foolish for you to sit moping here."

"Moping!" Mrs. Farley scoffed. Her throat shook. She gulped and her thin neck showed a corded undulation along its length.

"Well, what if you did see that Papa had a telegram from Mrs. Wilson? What of it? Is it anything new?"

Mrs. Farley's tight mouth puckered along the edges like fruit left too long in the sun. She stared resentfully at Alice. "New?" Mrs. Farley interrogated.

Alice took off her hat and whirled it in her hand. "I don't see why the fact that she happens to be passing through town makes the situation between you and Papa worse than it is all the time. You know the relation between them. It's gone on for twelve years now. She probably thinks her claim on him is just as good as yours."

For a moment the hard center of Mrs. Farley's vision dissolved in unshed tears and she saw Alice far off as in a vision of the dying.

"Why don't you quit this thing if you don't like it?" Alice went on. "You can come and live with me and leave Papa to do what he pleases."

Then Mrs. Farley's face went hard again with malice and fear, and her brow flushed with a streak like a whiplash. Her fingers had short, blunt, yellowish nails flecked with white. Her hands made impotent gestures. She was like a sheep searching for a gate when she must leap over a wall. "It's evident how little you understand your father," she said defiantly.

Alice gave a disagreeable laugh. She felt herself building her mother's world, sound like her own upon ramparts of pain.

"Your father has always felt that he had to make atonement for what he did—that no matter what kind of a woman Mrs. Wilson was that she——" Mrs. Farley could not go on.

"Well, he didn't have a child by her because he preferred you."

Mrs. Farley's whole face trembled with her sense of outrage and impotence. Her eyes, squinting a little, were those of a creature who takes no pride in its rage. "Whatever you say, I can't forget my duty to your father. I wish you had never heard of this! You're a coarse, cold woman, Alice."

Alice smiled, glad her mother had hurt her. "Yes,
you've told me that before."

They faced each other, Mrs. Farley trying to speak
but unable. Alice saw how ugly her mother was and
was ashamed of seeing it. Mrs. Farley turned her
head a little and there were spiked wisps of iron-gray
hair clinging on the nape of her scrawny, freckled neck.

"Let me go out!" Mrs. Farley said, stumbling suddenly toward the door in a blind gesture of protest and
escape.

"I'm not keeping you," Alice said.

"Everything would be well enough if you weren't bent
on persecuting me!" Mrs. Farley called back.

Alice was very calm. "I'm not persecuting you. If
you really prefer to go on this way, tied like a millstone
about Papa's neck, it is your own affair, I suppose;
though I can't help protesting when I see it."

Mrs. Farley was gone. Alice felt a kind of hysterical relief in her mother's exit.

*   *   *

It was a cool, delicate morning. The curtains swung
in the opened windows before the cool, darkened room.
The iron rails along the area made light black em-
broideries of shadow among blobs and flecks of gold on
the basement front. Even the tap of hoofs in the
street sounded as though the horses trod in hesitation.

In Mrs. Farley's dining-room light shivered against
the edges of knives and forks laid on the clean cloth,
and flew off in needle-fine sparks.

Laurence had gone, but Mr. Farley and Alice had just seated themselves at table. Mr. Farley was more abstracted and uncomfortable than usual.

"Isn't your mother well, Alice?" he asked in a low voice. "She hasn't sat down and last night she scarcely ate anything. I hate to see her spend so much time in the kitchen."

"She saw the telegram you dropped yesterday morning," Alice said.

Mr. Farley flushed and fine lines came between his eyes, but before he could say what hovered on his lips, Mrs. Farley came in and he was silent.

Mrs. Farley's arms were limp with the weight of the tray she carried. Her fingers clutched at the edges. There was something exasperating in her manner that suggested the senseless tremor of frightened canaries' wings. Her hands were unsteady and some of the contents of the coffee urn splashed on her wrist.

Alice got up. "Give me that tray." She took it firmly. "Now you sit down and eat."

"I—I've had something to eat," Mrs. Farley said weakly, at the same time sitting down.

Mr. Farley glanced at her but looked away quickly. He could not bear to see her fear which was like a fear of him. He cleared his throat. "Aren't you feeling well, Mother?"

Alice kept a rigorous gaze full of cruel pity steadily upon her mother's face.

"Why, yes—I——" She turned to Alice. "I have so much to do, Alice, I can't——" As she assisted her-

self to her feet, her flabby grip fell from the edge of the
table. She swayed a little. "I left the oven on."

"You sit down." Alice tried to push her back.

"No, no! I must turn it off." She brushed by and
left Alice looking after her.

Mr. Farley tried to be elaborately unmindful of by-
play and he pretended not to see his wife's wearily
bowed head and the palsied tremor of her thin neck.

As she went out, her shoulders rounded, her knees
loose, her head thrust forward, her feet dragging the
carpet, she left vividly the impression of her very thin
neck, taut and elongated, like the neck of a goose when
it attempts flight. She held her sharp elbows at right
angles to her sides with the same rigid anticipation of
haste.

"Has—has——" Mr. Farley could not bear to con-
fess to the actuality. "Couldn't you let her rest for
a week, Alice? You don't expect to get another position at once. As long as you are at home it seems to
me that you and I could combine to keep the house
going and let her off."

"She wouldn't do it. Pottering around consoles her
more than anything else."

There was silence. Mr. Farley gulped his coffee.
His face remained flushed and there were tears of discomfort in his eyes.

"*You* know what's the matter with Mamma, Father!"
Alice's subdued voice sounded to him almost threatening.

Mr. Farley gazed at his daughter helplessly. "Why,

no—I—no———" She looked so much like a startled
baby that Alice wanted to laugh.

"She knows Mrs. Wilson is in town and———"

Mr. Farley interrupted hurriedly. "But, my dear
child, I—I———" He moved his knife and fork nervously about.

Alice felt strong. Her frankness gave her the relief
which the maniac feels in his cruelty when he touches
flesh and it responds to him with sentience. "Don't
think I don't understand your situation, Father. I do.
I'm simply trying to look at it from Mamma's stand-
point."

He glanced up. Their eyes met. Alice had swung
back on the two rear legs of her chair, her coarse hand
on the edge of the table holding her steady. Her eyes
were self-righteously excited, her mouth harsh with determination.

To make him feel! She longed for that sympathetic
quiver. Darkness. Behind her thoughts, two sharp
strokes from the scissors let out the clotted honey of
pain, too sweet for the veins.

"Mamma doesn't really love you any more than you
love her, Papa."

Mr. Farley glanced nervously toward the kitchen
door. His features suddenly relaxed in the flaccidness
of self-pity. His eyes shone dimly. "I don't think you
realize the true satisfaction there is in duty well done,
Alice," he said shakily. "Things may be——— This is
no place to—to discuss details—but I would not know-
ingly hurt your mother for anything on earth."

Alice watched him narrowly and saw him loving himself in his tears. "I didn't suppose you'd have the courage to go out and commit murder—if that's what you mean," she said sharply. Her chair bumped against the floor and she stood up.

Mr. Farley was desperate. "There is more than one kind of perfectly genuine affection." His voice was unsteady. He drew lines and cross lines on the table cloth with his knife.

Alice laughed and tapped her foot on the floor. He was hurt by her laughing, but he would not look at her. He felt that he had allowed his parental advantage to escape him and he did not know how to reassert it.

Mrs. Farley, made uneasy by the murmur of monotonously subdued voices, was afraid to stay away any longer. She came in very intent on the plate of biscuits she carried, pretending that she considered nothing unusual afoot.

"The atmosphere of this moral cellar has ruined mine and Laurie's life!" Alice said angrily, as if driven to the words by the sight of her mother's face.

Mr. Farley was bewildered and angry. Mrs. Farley slipped the plate of biscuits to the table and sank weakly in a chair.

Mr. Farley rose. "I won't have you talk this way before your mother, Alice." In the depths of him he was profoundly alarmed, but on the surface he was sure of himself again.

Alice hated herself, but she stood at bay.

"I respect your mother," he said, "and you should do far more than respect her."

"I want to respect her, but she doesn't respect herself."

Mrs. Farley wept helplessly in silence.

"I won't have you insult her, Alice."

"I'm not insulting her. I'm not the one who takes it for granted that she is willing to go on forever and ever in this equivocal fashion. I've done her the honor of thinking she might be glad to separate from you and leave you free to live decently."

"I'll go away, Alice! I'll go away! My children don't love me!" Mrs. Farley squinted her lids together and, throwing back her head, wrung her hands abandonedly.

"Mother!" Mr. Farley laid a soothing hand on her mouse-gray hair, dry and silky like fur.

She moved away from him, shaking her hands. Her lids relaxed smoothly over her eyes and the tears coursed more easily through her worn lashes, and fell upon the nose glasses dangling from the gold hook on her breast. "You'll probably be glad I'm gone. Oh, my God, this is the reward of my life!"

"Hush, Mother! Hush! You're talking nonsense. Nobody even dreams of you going away. Why, it's preposterous."

"Alice says you want me to go!" she moaned.

"Alice doesn't know what she is talking about. I need you as much as you need me."

"But Alice wants me to go. My children don't want me!" She opened eyes that were blank with the abnormality of her passion. "You don't want me!"

"Mother!"

She struggled to her feet and brushed past him. He began to follow her, but halted half way to the door with an air of helpless indecision.

"I'm sorry, Papa," Alice said after a minute.

He could not answer. He put his hand to his head and walked away from her. For a moment he stood by the window with his hands over his eyes. At last he said, "It is cruel and useless to subject your mother to a thing like this—not to mention that I don't deserve it, Alice."

"I know it, Papa, but I hate to have to keep looking at the thing. You and Mamma are of no earthly use to each other, and it seems so stupid for you to sacrifice yourself to a lie like this."

Mr. Farley hung his head and smoothed his broad brow with slow trembling fingers. "Readjustments are expensive, Alice."

"I know they are, but you can't blame me for wanting to see things right."

They were silent. Mr. Farley was uncomfortable. He did not know what was expected of him. "You must try to comfort your mother," he said at last.

"She'll probably find some comfort for herself," Alice said bitterly.

"Well, I must go to the office. My first duty to her is there." Trying not to hurry, Mr. Farley, his face averted, walked out.

His back, as he disappeared through the doorway, looked stiff and weary. He seemed weak and humiliated like a big dog in pain.

*   *   *

At the noon hour Mrs. Farley came downstairs and shambled about the house, forcing herself on Alice's sight but refusing to speak. As Mrs. Farley's fingers fell into their wonted tasks the scene of the morning became less real to her than the feel of cloth and the posture of furniture. The habit of contentment crept back upon her. She wanted nothing of others. What should they want of her?

Dryly she preserved her already half-mummied antagonism.

*   *   *

On the glass windows that stretched, twinkling with light, across the broad front of the bakery and lunch room, the name was inscribed in a half moon of raised white letters. Behind the glass were mounds of iced cakes and piles of glossy yellow rolls resting in wooden trays.

A pink-faced German, with flat cheek bones, a stiff mustache, and narrow good-natured eyes, stood in his undershirt and trousers draped with a soiled apron, and laid out a new supply of cakes with alternate chocolate and white so that they formed a geometric pattern. Behind him on a rear wall a large clock marked six, the hands, on the stark white dial, rigid as the limbs of the crucified.

Above him lights glowed through globes of clouded glass. Groups of wagon drivers and workmen in gray jumpers sat at the tables and, leaning forward with chests to the marble tops, slopped coffee from their

saucers and shoveled huge accretions of potatoes and
meat into their mouths in the attitudes of hunting ani-
mals.

Outside, in the dusk, light spread hazily about the
lamps in the street. Over the roofs stars quivered delicately like fiery flowers of pale green on a shaken spray.

Old women crept along in the vague brightness, their
backs bent, parcels of half-wrapped bread and bits of
bloody meat held preciously to their shrunken breasts
or clutched in the knots of their shawls. A policeman,
leaning against a post, twirled his club and stared
smugly into the bright vacant faces of two pearl-rouged
girls in large black velvet hats.

Mrs. Farley, very genteel in her shabbiness, shrank
from the burly men and the rough children who ran
almost under her feet. But she felt superior to them
and the sight of them steadied her against life.

For years she had bought bread at the bakery. As
she went in the smell of baked bread floated against
her face like a palpable assurance of unchanging things.
But the memory of the morning's scene crept over her
like a coldness which she seemed to feel in the roots
of her hair. It was pain to feel the warmth of life
flowing away. Her coldness shuddered miserably
against the heat of the room.

"Some rolls, please. Fifteen cents' worth." Mrs.
Farley's smile was like the smile of the drowned, pale
through water. Her voice was so modulated that the
friendly blonde woman with her childlike eyes had to
lean from behind the counter and ask again what was
wanted.

Mrs. Farley waited for the rolls to be wrapped. The steam from the shining coffee urns enveloped her.

Every day for a dozen years. The world motionless in an atmosphere which held the gestures of the German baker and the big blonde woman with the smiling face.

Mrs. Farley walked home slowly. The bag of bread dangled in her cramped hand as she faced the chill wind blowing against her from the direction of her home—chill wind of strangeness.

Mr. Farley and Alice were in the house. Alice minded the children. Mr. Farley awaited his dinner.

To Mrs. Farley they were wild fish out of the sea caught in her glass. They were in the house making confident motions there as fish swim at their ease in an aquarium. They were terrible as the sea in a looking-glass.

Mrs. Farley mounted the front steps. Alice and Mr. Farley were a pain she would not admit. She shut them out. It should be night, and she would remain in the night where they meant nothing.

As she walked through the hall to the kitchen she felt strong again with the monotony of life. Beds, chairs, tables, walls rose strong about her. She made herself still like the walls.

*   *   *

Mrs. Farley pushed the bedroom door back. She did not speak.

Alice could barely distinguish the form which agi-

tated the darkness with its quiet. The two women felt
for each other through the gloom. They were like
water insects fumbling with antennæ.

"Mamma! Is that you?" Alice sat up straight in
bed.

Mrs. Farley, her heart beating unevenly, felt the
harsh stiffening of Alice's outline against the white blot
of the sheet.

Mrs. Farley tried to speak. She felt as though the
darkness were binding her lips with gray transparent
folds of shadow tough as silk. "Yes."

"What's the matter?" Alice threw the sheet back
and stood up on the floor. Half seen, she upreared
enormously like a wraith.

"Your father isn't home yet," Mrs. Farley said.

"Well, what of it?"

"I know where he is." Mrs. Farley's voice sounded
cracked.

"Then you ought not to worry."

"He's with that woman." Mrs. Farley's words
clacked like castanets in trembling hands; then fell
soundless.

Alice pitied her mother and grew hard. "Well, you
knew he was going to see her."

There was a silence. Then Mrs. Farley said, "I
know I can't expect any sympathy from you. My own
child connives with her father to get rid of me."

"I'm sorry things are like this, Mamma, but I won't
be blamed for them. If I were you I wouldn't allow
myself to be placed in this kind of a position."

"Oh, I know you! I know you!" Mrs. Farley's

voice broke as with age and vindictiveness. She turned
and went out, stumbling over the edge of the matting
and catching the door lintel as she passed into the
light.

Alice stood quietly a moment resisting the contagion
of her mother's panic. Then, conquering stubborn-
ness, she followed.

Mrs. Farley was in the back of the hall leaning
against the stair rail. She was in her nightdress that
fell, like hanging water, white through the gloom. She
was making a slow way toward the kitchen.

"What are you trying to do, Mamma?" Alice called.
Her body, uncorseted, was heavy. She walked quickly
after her mother. She knew what her mother was
trying to do.

Mrs. Farley dallied a little, but she would not answer. Her hands were hid, carrying something.

Alice came up behind. She caught her mother
quickly from the back. "Give me that pistol, do you
hear me!"

"No, no! I won't!" The scrawny body bent forward and doubled itself against Alice's reaching hand.

"Give it here." Alice was quiet and sure with excitement. Her big breast heaved under her loose nightgown. Her hair was tumbled about and her coarse
face was red with effort.

"Let me! Then you and your father can do what
you please!"

"Rubbish. Let it go, I say." Alice's fingers were
on the gun. Its hardness and coldness reassured her
of she knew not what.

She wanted to hurt me, Alice thought. What other reason did she have for coming to me about it?

"Oh, oh! You hurt my wrist!"

Alice clutched her mother's fingers and was cruel to them. The strong fingers pressed and twisted, still stronger. "Give me that gun!"

It dropped with a dull clatter on the bare floor.

Mrs. Farley's power over others was her power to hurt herself. Now it was gone. She was feeble.

"You try to get your father to leave me. You want to see me left here without anything and you won't let me kill myself," she hiccoughed, beginning to cry.

The gaslight on the wall was turned low. Alice reached for the screw and sent the flame up so that a yellow flood swept the shadows away.

Mrs. Farley's tear-inflamed eyes squinted at the light. She huddled against the wall. Her gray hair, undone, clung to her bare neck above her open nightdress. Her eyes, lifted to Alice, were opaque with misery.

Below her nightdress her feet were bare. Her toes with bulbous joints rested flaccid on the scrap of brown carpet at the head of the stair. She turned away from Alice and began to fumble blindly for the rail.

"Where are you going?"

Mrs. Farley slid herself feebly along the rail and down the first step. "I don't know! I don't know!" she wailed.

"Stop acting like that, Mamma. You know you can stand up."

"I can't! I can't! I don't care what becomes of me!"

Alice caught her mother in a grasp of repugnance and pulled her back. "You've got to brace up. You don't care what I think of you or what you do to me, but you have to have a little pride and a sense of responsibility toward Bobby and May. You can't let them see a thing like this. Is Laurence home yet?"

"No, he's not home. Why should I feel responsible for Bobby and May? You think I'm not fit for them. You want to take them away from me."

"I'm not going to pamper you by arguing with you. If I seriously thought that you wanted to end your life I should consider that interference was none of my business, but——"

"And yet you expect me to live! None of your business! Oh, my God!"

"But as you have no real intention of killing yourself you have no right to subject me to a scene like this. I want a little peace."

"A little peace! Oh, my God, a little peace!" Mrs. Farley shut her eyes and let her head fall backward and forward limply as though there were no vertebræ in her neck.

Alice shook her. "Stop it, Mamma."

Mrs. Farley rocked herself like a drunken woman. Finally, her eyes yet closed, she shuddered and was still.

"Are you calm now?"

"Yes. I'm calm. Whatever I do makes no differ-

ence to you. Nothing I do affects you. You're hard
as nails."

"We won't talk about that. You can affect me,
but because that is just what you want to do I'm not
going to let you."

"I want to do! She says I want to do!"

"I have to talk you into a state of common sense."

Still Mrs. Farley's head nodded as if with sleep and
her eyes remained shut. "Common sense. Yes, common sense," she repeated like a dream.

"Echoing me in that stupid way won't keep me from
going on."

"Stupid? She calls it a stupid way. My God! My
God! What agony!" Mrs. Farley almost shrieked
out "agony." Her knotted hands clutched her flat
breasts as if with hunger. Her voice was dully intense.
Her wrinkled lids twitched.

Why does she twitch her face?

Alice's lips curled almost like a snarl. "You'll find
me giving away and raving too if you don't watch out,
Mamma. I can't stand too much of this."

Mrs. Farley opened her eyes slowly, but she kept
her gaze vague against the solid antagonism of Alice's
eyes. "I'm going back to my room now. I can't sleep,
but I won't burden you any longer with the sight of
me. You can tell your father I'm not going to trouble
him any more. He can start his proceedings for divorce. I don't know what the Prices will say—what
they will think. They probably imagined just as I
did that the whole thing was over twelve years ago when
I went through so much humiliation to save your father.

It took the diabolical vileness of my own daughter to draw her father and this woman together again after we had a happy home and were all at peace."

"I didn't have a happy home. Papa hasn't a happy home."

"I know I'm vile. Guilty of all manner of vileness. It was vile of me to slave and work as I've done and take all of the responsibility off Laurence's hands and slave for Winnie and the children."

"I have nothing to do with Winnie and the children."

"I don't know what charge your father can bring. Then as soon as he gets it he can rush off and marry that thing. To judge by the way she was going when I saw her she must be middle-aged and fat by now, but your father won't mind so long as she's not me. Then my daughter will be freed of me. Winnie and Laurence can get somebody else to fetch and carry and clean up for their children. As you say, I have no right here. I ought not to be alive. But you can tell your father how it is and he'll find a way to get rid of me."

Alice was still like a mountain. "That's all right, Mamma. I'll tell Papa what you say—that you are willing for him to arrange for a divorce. Is that all right?"

"That's it! That's it! Let him arrange it anyway he will and don't have too much consideration for my feelings. Let him tell the judge that I've worn out my good looks so I don't attract him any longer."

Alice had heard the door slam below stairs. She stared at her mother's unconscious face and said nothing.

Mrs. Farley, dragging her feet exaggeratedly, moved off into her bedroom.

Then Alice pattered quickly down the stairs and met her father in the hall. He had heard voices and looked alarmed.

"Is anything the matter?" he asked, seeing her face angry and elated, and that she wore only her nightgown.

"Yes. Come into the living-room," Alice said.

They walked in. Mr. Farley was a long time finding the light. He felt choked by the guilty beating of his heart. When he had made the room bright he turned to Alice almost in fear. She looked so ugly, flushed, with her hair in confusion, and her angry eyes.

"I've been talking to Mamma," Alice said breathlessly.

Mr. Farley's face was drawn. He blinked at the light, gaining time. "I asked you not to talk to your mother," he said uncomfortably.

"I know you did, but she talked to me and I couldn't keep my mouth shut. She began by saying she knew where you had gone. She says she's willing to agree to a divorce."

Mr. Farley did not know what to say. The situation had been forced upon him unaware and he did not know what to do with it. "This is nonsense, Alice. Your mother knows that." He held his brow with his hand.

"Why is it nonsense? You've given up most of your life to her, but I don't see why you should keep on doing it!"

Mr. Farley could not understand what was happening, nor how it was he felt borne forward on an invisible current that flowed from Alice. He walked up and down the room. "You mustn't start these things, Alice."

Alice watched him contemptuously. "Don't blame me for the nightmare of lies and hypocrisy that exists between you and Mamma."

Mr. Farley kept rubbing his head. Then he walked stealthily to the hall door and closed it. His eyes, as he lifted them to Alice's face, had the blind awareness of a sheep's. He seemed to know all and to perceive nothing. "You mustn't misunderstand me, Alice. It is true that a satisfying companionship cannot exist between me and your mother, but she and I have made compromises for each other that have made it possible for us to live, and I can't think lightly of hurting her."

They were silent. Mr. Farley shaded his eyes with an unsteady hand.

"You did go to see Mrs. Wilson tonight, didn't you?" Alice asked after a minute.

"Yes. She is passing through town. I hadn't seen her for three years."

"My God! You don't need to apologize for it!"

They were quiet again.

"So you don't want to accept anything from Mamma even if she is willing to give?"

"You don't understand, Alice. That very fact makes me even more responsible for my own resolutions." His voice shook.

"Look here, Papa, I always imagined you had sacrificed yourself outright to Mamma's weakness and dependency, and now when you have a chance to get away from her and live with somebody who is younger whom you seem to care for, you actually seem to be dodging the issue just as though you were contented with your situation."

"You must remember that Mrs. Wilson must be considered—that what I selfishly want——" He stopped. Patiently through all these years he had strained forward like an animal pulling a loaded cart and, now the cart was being taken from him, he was disconcerted to find himself still straining forward pulling at nothingness. Bewildered, he tried to save his ideal of himself. "You must remember we have never really considered a divorce possible."

"Well, Papa, of course I can't decide your life for you. If you don't feel that you owe it to your son——" She turned resolutely.

He felt her scorn. He hated her, but he could not bear to have her go. He covered his face.

She walked out.

He could hear her run up the stairs, her bare feet making a soft sound. He wanted to call her back, but he did not know what to say. It was necessary to him to think well of himself.

*   *   *

Mrs. Farley went about her housework with renewed determination. She would speak to no one but Laurence. At the table she served them all, but if there was any general talk she did not hear it.

Mr. Farley grew into the habit of giving her furtive looks. He forgot to eat. He talked mostly to Bobby and May.

The weather was quite mild, but Mrs. Farley took to wearing an old red cashmere shawl and pulling it tight about her throat. When her husband or her daughter sought her averted gaze she wrapped herself tighter and shivered ostentatiously.

Bobby was too young to note changes which did not directly affect his interest, but May, with her shining eyes of a little stuffed goat, ruminated in her own way on what was making her grandmother eccentric. The little girl's pale lips parted loosely in wonder, as, ignoring her food, she watched her grandmother's oblivious face bent over the coffee.

Mrs. Farley was conscious of this all-absorbing gaze which had in it neither approval nor condemnation. She felt at a disadvantage before the child, and, when May asked for anything, found it difficult not to push her away with expressions of violence.

Laurence saw that something was wrong again between his parents. Alice with her damned interference, he told himself.

When his mother spoke to him his voice was gentle. But he could not endure other people's pain. He kept away from her as much as possible.

In this web of silence between her father and mother Alice felt herself caught by threads of iron. She could not move.

One morning when she and her mother were alone

Alice said, "I told Papa that you were willing for him
to arrange a divorce."

Mrs. Farley's face, in its deliberated vagueness,
quivered like a gray jelly, but she kept her eyes away
and her body did not quicken to more expressive life.

"Yes. I supposed you did. I suppose by now the
two of you have fixed it up."

"You'll have to talk sensibly about it or he can't
do it."

Mrs. Farley gave Alice one weak terrible look.

Alice could not bear the look. To get away from it
and from a desire to do something violent she walked
into the living-room.

*   *   *

The children were playing in the back yard when
Bobby fell down and hurt himself. May sat flat on
the grass before the sandpile, but when she saw that
Bobby was hurt she struggled to her feet on her thin
legs like a weak young colt, and went to help him.

"You're full of dirt." She squatted before him
brushing his clothes, her stiff petticoats tilted up in
front, her buttocks, in small soiled drawers, swinging
close to the earth.

Just then Aunt Alice came out of the kitchen door
and stood on the step. In the sunshine her bare hair
showed a burnt brown. The wind whipped her heavy
skirts against her stout thighs. She saw Bobby crying
with his mouth open and his eyes shut, trying to squeeze
the tears from between his lids.

"Hush that, Bobby! Aren't you ashamed of your-self?"

Bobby cried louder. When she came down the path her undeviating approach made him mad with passion. "Dow 'way!" he shouted. When Aunt Alice reached him he pounded against her stomach with his fists.

She clasped his plump wrists folded in fat and held them while he struggled until the dirt and sweat with which they were grimed rolled up under her fingers. At this moment she loved him more intensely because she could hurt him.

"Dow 'way!" he kept shouting. His hair was tumbled about his face. He was red with passion. When he had freed himself he ran toward the house. "I hate Aunt Alice! I hate Aunt Alice! I wants my dranma!" he called back.

With sudden confidence, May sidled toward her aunt. "We've been makin' mud pies and coverin' 'em with sand like icin'," she said.

Alice looked down. Pale. May's hair shining like a dead sun. Alice all at once hated May's hair because it was pale and bright. "It's too chilly to make mud pies. For Heaven's sake don't put your dirty hands on me, May!" With a violent push Alice put the little girl aside and walked briskly up the path.

A few surprised tears trickled from the resigned and shining misery of May's eyes. She watched her aunt move toward the house.

Conscious of May's pale hair floating after her in unsubstantial brightness, Alice rushed up the stairs to her room. She pulled down the shades, longing for the heaviness of dark. The room in shadow was a pool on which Alice's unhappiness, dreamy and intermittent, floated like a swamp light.

Outside the softness of the room, where solitude allowed her to relax, the soul of her family surrounded her, rearing its ramparts of towers beaten in the iron of years.

Where will my light go to? Ugly old maid. Emancipation of women. Why did I not tell him that I loved him?

Darkness floated from her words.

*   *   *

The morning was gray. The windows along the street were fathomlessly blank. Across the asphalt wet wheel tracks stretched glistening and sinuous like black rubber snakes.

Mr. Farley stepped into the street and closed the front door stealthily behind him. Too agitated to endure breakfast with his family, he remembered the cheap restaurant around the corner, a place lined with grotesque mirrors and white and narrow like the corridor of a ship.

When he went in he found the floor, covered with brick-colored linoleum, smeared and darkened with grease, and the cloth on the table where he seated himself was stained with pink-brown splashes of wine. The waiter came up, a soft heavy man whose feet pressed the floor as soundlessly as those of a panther. Mr. Farley took the list of dishes from the waiter's hand, fat like the hand of a corpse. The waiter's sad little eyes were set in a broad white face stubbled with bluish beard. When he moved away he was like a ghost. His large hips swayed, woman-wise. His soiled apron floated over a generous belly as profound as sleep.

Flies buzzed against the walls and fell back upon the half-washed table coverings and the cracked cruets opaque from many fillings.

Mr. Farley stirred gray crystals of sugar into the gold-edged blackness of his coffee, then clouded it with the pale blue-auraed milk that brimmed the squat white pitcher.

He tried to think things out, but he had nurtured his self-esteem on the verity of abnegation and it was hard for him to accept as a blessing the thing which it had given him so much comfort to do without.

Safe in the conviction that there would be no end to his sacrifice, he had allowed full abandon to his mystical and repressed nature. Helen Wilson had become glorified and beyond attainment. He was in terror of seeing her too clearly. When her neat figure, a little stout, emerged distinctly from the chaos of his reflections, he deliberately let down a curtain of confusion across the mirror of his consciousness.

*   *   *

After dinner Mr. Farley went into the living-room and seated himself in an armchair. He had scarcely exchanged a word with any one during the meal. He bent his head in his hands. The light from the shaded lamp glistened obliquely along the thin parting of his hair and his baldish scalp.

Mrs. Farley made pretexts to come near him. In the afternoon she had been mending a nightdress of May's and left it on top of the magazine rack, and now she came to get it.

She was a long time putting her sewing things together. Mr. Farley saw her, but he did not stir.

Alice had followed her mother into the room and halted abruptly behind her.

Mrs. Farley did not see Alice. Mr. Farley started a little, glanced at his daughter, and looked away again.

Alice, watching the two people, felt the atmosphere of the room weighted with inertias. These people forced her back into herself, into her own dumbness. She wanted to shatter her silence with their cries.

"Turn around here and look at Papa, Mamma," Alice said suddenly.

Mrs. Farley would not look. "Your father knows what I think," she said after a minute. She glanced at Alice.

Mrs. Farley wore her pince-nez and the irridescence of glass added remoteness to her hostile uneasy eyes. The gold clasp drawing the flesh together on her nose gave a twist of severity to her dry obscure face. Her hate seemed to flow uncertainly through the crystals and flash defiance in the gold center. The little gold clasp of the pince-nez was like the claw of impotence buried in its own flesh.

Alice tapped the floor with her foot. "Do you know what Mamma thinks, Papa? I'm sure I don't."

Mr. Farley stared under his fingers at the floor where the dim pattern of the carpet grew more dim. "I know what you have told me."

"I can't stand the atmosphere here. If you and she don't find some way to talk it out you'll drive Laurence and me insane."

Mr. Farley sighed deeply. "I'm ready and willing to discuss anything. I have felt lately that I have become an intruder in your mother's eyes, but I hardly know what has happened, Alice."

Mrs. Farley glanced at the bright baldish spot in her husband's scalp. It seemed to her the center of the unreality in which she had existed of late, and she was as if held together by the grip of the glasses on her nose, the one tense and sure sensation which contradicted her feeling of dispersion. Then she looked at Alice.

"I can't leave May and Bobby upstairs alone even to talk things over." She pulled the red shawl about her neck and started for the door. "It seems to me you and your father have settled my life for me, anyway," she called back.

Mr. Farley did not move for a moment after her exit. Then he stood up, and, making a hopeless gesture with his hands, walked out in silence, shaking his head.

His thoughts were eddying in a current which sucked down his self-esteem. He wanted to give back her happiness to his wife that it might make him beautiful in his own eyes. He wanted the cool peace of purchased misery.

Alice, left alone, was hot and futile.

I shall go out of me in dark blood.

She walked to the window. The street was empty. Over the blue-bright housetops, the quiet sky and the cold moon. She leaned her forehead against the glass and looked into the street.

She felt suddenly tired, endless, capable of giving birth to endless selves. She was tired. She could not die. She was like a mother bearing herself forever like endless children.

PART III

THERE was a blacksmith's forge down the road by the farmhouse where Winnie and her mother were staying. In the morning in the silence the first sound Winnie heard was the chiming of the hammer like a bell.

There were maple trees against her window. The leaves were yellowing. When the sun shone through them they were a silken veil of light.

The days were long and bright. The farmer's wife was busy with household tasks and Winnie and her mother spent uninterrupted hours on the long narrow veranda when Mrs. Price embroidered, or read a novel while Winnie listened.

Winnie was oppressed by the silence. She had not cared at first to believe that she would have a child, but the dark thought ran along after her like a dog that will not be beaten off. She knew it was there in her mind, but she would not recognize it.

Dr. Beach came into the country to visit her. He spoke of the care she must give to her health and he told her that if she continued to improve over a long time she might be able to evade the operation.

It was only when he gave her hope that despair forced her to realize herself. She gazed at him in helpless terror. When he turned to speak to her mother, Winnie left the room, and while he remained she did not come back.

After the doctor had gone Mrs. Price entered the old-fashioned farm bedroom and found Winnie lying on her face.

"Winnie! My darling! You are sobbing your heart out!" Mrs. Price's black-clothed body trembled and her precise voice shook. She laid her blue-veined hand on Winnie's wrist.

But Winnie could not tell. She glanced up, her little face dim with despair.

"Winnie! Are you in pain? Shall I call the doctor again? Winnie, my darling! Dear child, answer me! You must not act like this!"

But Winnie buried her head in pillows and would not reply. She had wept out all she wanted to say. She was sodden. She was still. There was nothing left in her but silence.

Mrs. Price, tears of anxiety in her eyes, gripped Winnie's wrists and held them tight. They were still together. The wooden clock ticked on the low mantel. Then Mrs. Price said, "Winnie, if you cannot manage to tell me what is the matter I shall telegraph your father."

Crushed against Mrs. Price's finality, Winnie struggled to free herself. "I want to die! Oh, I want to die!" she said, and every time she said "die," something in her shouted against the dumbness of her throat, life, life! The shriek was against Laurence and against the living child that had come to consume her.

Mrs. Price shivered as with cold, but she tried to be calm. "Winnie," speaking very low, "you *must* use some self-control. Something terrible has happened. You have heard something from home which you have not told me. I am your mother. I love you better than anything in the world, and you have no right to keep me in ignorance of anything that is troubling you." Her lips were bluish and her upper lip was wet with sweat. The skin on her hands was withered like white crêpe and the veins swelled in her trembling wrists.

The clock ticked. Winnie murmured something in the pillow. Mrs. Price waited.

Outside the open window the evening air congealed in heaviness. It hung cold and bitter over the moist grass. The smell of weeds floated into the room.

Mrs. Price looked out and saw that each stalk of golden rod in the meadow opposite was separately still. The sky was blue stone. Only the pine trees seemed warm against the vacuous shining of twilight. For night was terrible, descending in brightness. It was a mirror in the pale still sky. It was nothing.

Slowly the darkness grew up from the earth, and, as the trees darkened, the earth began to grow into being.

Winnie was glad of the darkness. When the room grew dark she did not hold the child separately in her body. It lay with her in the body of the dark and she was freed of it.

"Mamma!" She sat up, her body a harsh gray stroke of determination against the white inert pillow.

"Yes, my dear." Mrs. Price smoothed her child's brow. "Oh, I am so glad you are quieter, Winnie."

Out of the silence from which the sun had passed
the moon suddenly unrolled, huge and white and dry
as a dead flower. A dragon-fly darting across the
window and the dry white face of the moon, so gorgeously lifeless, was a gold thorn sinking into the quiet
flesh of shadow.

Voices sounded from the road. The lowest branches
of the trees yet trembled with light. Then the world
died away in the chirping of insects and the bleat of
frogs.

"I will light a lamp, darling." Mrs. Price went over
to a table. She could barely be seen. The match
spurted suddenly into flame, and she was plain again.

When the lamp was lit the night outside went
black and the moon, now vast and green and strange,
rushed gorgeously against the lifted window pane.

Lamplight sucked at the shadows but could not draw
them utterly to itself so that the corners of the big
room remained vague and only here and there some
object gave out a grudging glint.

Mrs. Price was stiff but shaken and gentle. "Now,
Winnie, darling, tell me what has made you like this."
She came to the bed and looked down.

Winnie threw back her head and, with closed eyes,
plucked at the bedclothes. "I can't tell you."

"Are you unhappy? Has something happened between you and your husband, my child? You must
be fair to me, Winnie."

Winnie rocked herself. "Oh, I can't tell. What
would be the use? I can't tell."

"What am I to do, Winnie?"

Still Winnie rocked herself. "Oh, I would rather be dead!" she said.

"Don't say that, Winnie! We mustn't think such thoughts. Aren't we doing everything on earth to make you live? Your father and I want to do everything on earth to make life better and surer and sweeter for you and your babies."

Winnie began to throw herself about in the bed again. "Oh, I'd rather be dead than to be sick and have another baby. I know I'm going to die."

"Have another baby." Mrs. Price did not receive the words. They were strange. They remained outside her.

Then, all at once, without her being aware of the moment, their meaning entered into her and burnt her with terror.

"What do you mean, Winnie? This isn't possible." Mrs. Price seated herself shakily on the bed and took Winnie's struggling hands again. "Ba—— This is nonsense, Winnie." She held Winnie's hands firmly. Her own hands were dry and hot.

Mrs. Price felt strange with herself. The words had changed her. She was in a new place.

"How long has this——" She tried to speak. Her throat was dry. She could not go on.

"Oh, don't ask me—six weeks—two months—I don't know!"

"Winnie, are you sure of this?"

"I'm sure of it."

Mrs. Price's grip on Winnie's arms relaxed. Winnie lay still, moaning.

Mrs. Price got up. Her eyes looked wasted with fear. She stared helplessly at her daughter.

"Oh, Winnie, what shall I do for you?"

Winnie's nostrils, very wide open, quivered like those of a mare crazy with a painful bit. "I won't! I'll die first!" she said. "I won't!"

Laurence was around her, in her, formless like smoke. Her animosity to him was living its separate life within her.

She sobbed herself into numbness. She would not feel it. She wanted the life in her to lie cold and numb. Her breasts swelled. She thought she could feel the milk flowing through them like shame through her flesh.

Mrs. Price walked up and down the room, clasping and unclasping her hands. "Yes, I'll send for Dr. Beach. We must send for Dr. Beach. I cannot understand your husband, Winnie."

Bewildered by the catastrophe as she was, it gave her a certain feeling of assurance to be able unreservedly to condemn Laurence again.

She gazed at Winnie prone on the bed and felt suddenly sickened with futility. All of Mrs. Price sickened and armed against Laurence. She wanted to snatch the child from the taint of its father as from a disease.

"Why didn't you tell me this sooner, Winnie? Something might have been done. You know how unwise this is in your state."

Winnie stared at her mother. "I'm going to die."

Again tears swam in Mrs. Price's eyes, but she would

not unbend herself. "No, dear, you are not going to die. We will take good care of you and you will come through this terrible thing."

Winnie stirred wearily and impatiently. "I don't care. I'm going to die." She was stubborn and calm now. Die was a stupid word like dust. It settled dully upon her pain.

* * *

Mrs. Price wrote a letter to Mrs. Farley. "Winnie is evidently going to have another baby. This is a great misfortune. I cannot understand how Laurence allowed this to occur. In her state you may imagine!"

It was apparent that Mrs. Price was alarmed and that in writing the letter her hand had trembled, but it was plain too that in her veiled reproaches she was still delicately gratifying her hatred of Laurence.

* * *

Winnie, waiting for Dr. Beach, refused to stay in bed. She got up and put on a flowered négligé and sat by the open window. Looking down the long wet road, she hated the hill that set itself up heavily between her and the sky. She hated life that came to the end of itself abruptly like the road to the horizon at the end of the hill.

When Dr. Beach came in Winnie spoke to him resentfully, and when her mother told him what was the matter, blushed a defiant crimson.

It was a delicate situation to consider. All three people thought of Laurence with condemnation, but mention of him was eschewed. When Mrs. Price talked her voice was choked with pent opprobrium.

Dr. Beach told Winnie to undo her dressing gown. When he examined her, his hot hands touched her cold body here and there lightly.

She felt her body harshen to his touch. It was at the moment when his hand touched her that the child became hers. It was not that she wanted the child, but that she wanted the thing the man could not touch. She hated the day when the child would no longer be secret.

After the doctor had touched her and made her aware of the child she ceased in part to feel that Laurence was in the child's flesh. She would have liked to think of herself as the only creature capable of giving birth.

Dr. Beach was uncomfortable. He talked vaguely. He had advised her against having a child, but because it would have been better to avoid this contingency there was no reason to suppose she would not pull through all right. "Above all," he told Mrs. Price, "keep her mind off herself. Do not allow her to become depressed."

*   *   *

Nearly four months had passed while Winnie remained in the country with her mother. Autumn was at a close.

One day Winnie felt her flesh move. This quicken-

ing was as though she had never before known herself
with child. She conjectured for the first time all of
the inevitable details of the baby's birth. There was
nothing to speculate. She felt herself caught in the
grip of this horrible sameness.

One Sunday Mr. Price came down from town to see
them. He had the air of a victor, and Mrs. Price,
who was conquering the exultance of her resentment
toward Laurence, felt guilty in understanding her husband's secret content.

"That man ought to be killed!" Mr. Price said to
his wife. "He ought to be strung up and tarred and
feathered. Nothing is too severe to do to a fellow like
that. I suppose you'll say that for Winnie's sake we
must keep our hands off."

Mrs. Price was agitated. "Oh, yes, we must try
to keep the peace for Winnie's sake. You must remember, Perry, this is a hard time for her."

Mr. Price walked back and forth across the room,
flapping his coat-tails with his hands and blowing out
his mustache. "I should say it was! I should say it
was!" he repeated. He had his head lowered like that
of a bull about to charge, and in the depths of his
murky blue eyes glowed a surreptitious spark of triumph. "Bad blood in that Farley family," he said.

Winnie came into the room reluctantly, prepared to
resist her father's bullying. Her soft eyes were hard
with reserves.

Mr. Price came up to her and gave her a dominating
caress. "Well, Winifred, how are you, my dear little
girl?"

She returned his perfunctory kiss, her moist lips cool with distaste.

"Feeling pretty badly, dear?"

"No, Father. I'm feeling pretty well."

He cleared his throat. He was disappointed.

"I ought to be going home," Winnie pouted, smiling a little, "but Mother won't let me. I had letters from Laurie and Mamma Farley just to-day and they are worried about me."

"Worried about you! So are we worried about you! I'd like to know where home is if it's not right here with your mother! Your own mother is certainly the one to take care of you when you're in this state!"

"Mamma Farley took care of me when my other two babies were born," Winnie said stiffly.

Mr. Price choked, and to relieve himself, went to the window and spit.

Mrs. Price began to speak tremulously for his comfort. "Those were circumstances we couldn't help, dear. Thank Heaven that this time, when you are really more seriously in need of us, we are here beside you to do everything in our power. I think Winnie ought to lie down and rest," Mrs. Price said, shepherding her husband out of the room before his exultance should become too crass.

*   *   *

Laurence came heavily into the house and hung up his hat. All day he had felt the new child, a fiery thread through the blackness of his mind sewing him to earth. His fear of the new child smoldered like a hot ache in the back of his brain.

Thirty-one years old. He could not bear to recall in detail the incidents of his life. He had achieved nothing; so he had ceased to believe in achievement. As a boy he had invariably thought of himself in grandiose and ultra-masculine rôles. When girls had come into his dreams they had come in gratitude to receive some contemptuous beneficence at his hands. He was ashamed now when he recalled the gauche sense of superiority that had showed itself in bad manners. And yet his habit of mind remained the same. When he ceased to give himself he would admit equality, and he could not do that. His pride bound him to endless obligations. Against Winnie, he obliterated gladness in himself and denied his acquisitive spirit. She should have him all and he would be nothing.

The door in the hall opened behind Laurence and closed with a sharp click of the latch. Laurence moved in the heaviness of circles, but Alice's movements were always angular and resistent.

"Hello, Laurie," she said coldly. They seldom talked together.

The gas flame burnt blue in the cold hall. Alice took off her beaver sailor hat and hung it beside Laurence's acid-stained derby.

She looked at him. The patience she read in his coarse florid face was like everything else in the house. The house at night was a monstrous phlegmatic beast half drowned. Its inmates were sightless parasites.

Alice was pugnacious. "What's the matter with

you?" she joked brusquely. "Winnie hasn't had twins, has she?"

"Winnie's all right," Laurence said.

"How do you regard the prospect of becoming a proud father a third time, Laurence?" she demanded suddenly. She knew she was offensive but felt she must wrench something from this huge mass of bitterly desponding flesh.

The world was muted with fleshiness and heaviness. Only in her own body pain rang clear and sharp and chiming sweet. Her pain was her beauty that she kept inside herself. It was her virginity. She felt that he had no beauty of pain.

"You are the only thing that reconciles me to it, Alice," he retorted sourly.

"A benighted old spinster, eh?"

"Well, I have a pretty wife and shall soon have three lovely children. My state has its compensatory illusions."

"Ah, yes, I suppose it has." She did not know what more to say to him. He walked into the living-room, ignoring her.

It was a moment before she could make herself follow him.

If Winnie died—— How did these things happen? Laurence was almost like a murderer.

For a moment she envied him, then in her terrible emptiness she felt herself more beautiful than he.

Mad. I'm going mad. He doesn't know.

Laurence wanted to get away from her. His expression of life was always bitter and cheap and he knew it, but he was rather proud of the exquisiteness which made it unendurable for him to tell the truth to himself. He despised Alice for the brutal veracity of her introspection. Alice carried pain of self like a banner. He felt that her arrogant suffering showed a want of fineness. To dare to see as she did, he felt, one must be emotionally dull.

Winnie was false and puerile, but because he felt that the truth would kill Winnie, she seemed to him more delicate and beautiful than Alice.

Alice recognized that Laurence hated her because she understood him too well.

She could not comprehend this. She would have let herself be known even in utter contempt. She was clouded now with the murk of herself that no one would know. She wanted to be known to be cleansed.

*　　*　　*

Winnie was tired of the country that left her too much with herself. She hated the empty road in the bleak days and the black tree at the end that swayed against the damp green twilights. She was glad when Mrs. Price agreed that it was time for them to go back to the city.

They left the farmhouse at night. Mr. Price had sent his car out and in it they were driven to the station, ten miles away. It was moonlight. The pine trees along the road tossed their green hair in the wind. The long boughs swept the ground. The trees clutched the earth with their roots as if in a frenzy. They would not give way.

At the deserted station one light burned over the window where the telegraph operator worked. They sat for a long time in the dim waiting room, until the big train, fiery and terrible, rushed out of nothing and came to a standstill at the end of the platform.

When they went into the long dim car hung with green curtains, every one was asleep.

Mrs. Price helped her daughter to undress and Winnie lay down on her side in the lower berth with the window shade up. As she lay there and the train began to move, the oppression of the last few weeks culminated in her emotions, in an unreasoning panic, and she imagined that she was already dead.

It was foggy. The train passed through a railway yard and Winnie saw rows of empty cars, long and low, that were like monsters with lusterless hides and opaque eyes, submerged in mist. Hundreds of dull eyes stared from the dimly shining windows, the pale eyes of the cars.

Delicate bridges floated over her head as the train passed beneath them, and the swinging arms of derricks and huge machines, lifted through the mist, were as frail as lace.

Lights burst against the mist like rotted stars, and there were other lights that opened upon her suddenly, glad and unseeing as the eyes of blind men raised in delight.

The moon, small with distance, slimed over with fog, was green like money lost a long time. The telegraph wires stretched across the pale landscape tautly, like harpstrings. One after another the flat branched poles seemed to open submissive palms to the passing train.

Winnie wanted the morning. She wanted to get back to Mamma Farley and her familiar commonplace. Before expanding in voluptuous rebellion, Winnie wanted to know that the cage was sure. Somehow Mamma Farley made her more certain of its sureness.

In the morning they alighted in the teeming station, and Winnie, anxious not to be seen, walked a little behind Mrs. Price. Winnie was ashamed of herself. She felt herself cold and isolated in the vividness of the life she contained.

At the big gate at the end of the track, they met Laurence. "Well, Winnie. Well, Mrs. Price."

Winnie looked up at him with eyes shuddering in softness. She showed him her helplessness against which he could not defend himself. When she lifted her mouth he had to kiss her. She was ashamed of his shabby clothes.

Laurence tried to say something to Mrs. Price. "You look well."

"Yes, and Winnie has gotten along very nicely with me. How is your mother? How are the children?" She did not look at him, and while she talked she moistened her lips that were like paper under her tongue.

In the waiting room they met Mr. Price. He had arrived at the train a few moments late and the confusion of the incoming crowd had carried them past him before he knew it.

He was gruff and short with Laurence. "How-do,
Farley?" He turned quickly to Winnie. "Well,
Winnie, you're back, are you? How is she, Vivien?
Mother and I are going to keep a tight hold on you,
my young lady. We are going to see that your health
is taken care of after this."

"You'll let us take you and Winnie home in the carriage?" Mrs. Price said to Laurence.

"I have a taxicab for Winnie, Mrs. Price." He took
Winnie's arm. She protested a little.

"It seems so absurd," Mrs. Price demurred, preserv-
ing her well-bred poise, but plainly irritated.

Laurence, pretending not to hear, dragged Winnie
on.

Winnie pouted and hung back. "You'll come to see
me this afternoon, Mother," she called over her shoulder.

Mrs. Price nodded and smiled.

*   *   *

It was Sunday. Winnie had fallen sick, and, to
escape the feeling of tension that prevailed at home,
Laurence went into the country for a long walk.

Winnie might die. Then what? In the sense of
oppression he experienced, the thought of Winnie's
danger awoke something in him which he refused to
recognize, which was like a stealthy and terrible hope
of relief.

He walked on, immersed in himself, scarcely real-
izing that he moved. Then the ardor of his imaginings

subsided in the familiar contours of being and he saw
the road again, stretching before him like a shadowed
light and the pale trees standing away on either side
against the dim enormous sky.

Laurence wondered if he had grown suddenly old.
Formerly, without articulating it, he had experienced
a sense of immanence on every hand. Now he felt dry
and exhausted in his nameless understanding. Everything remained outside him. He had lost the power of
enlarging his being. From his numbness he regarded
enviously what he considered the illusions of others,
and yet his exhaustion seemed to him the sum of life
and he could not but consider with contempt all those
who imagined that there was anything further.

Only the horror that was between Winnie and himself gave him a little life. The hideousness of his father-
hood made his apathy glow a little like an illumined
grimace. Through sheer irrelevance it seemed to have
some meaning. He began to depend on this ugly fact
of the child he did not want.

Yet he could not bear to be in the sickroom where
Winnie was. Her sweetly pathetic commonplace was
so grotesquely familiar that he could scarcely endure
to be aware of it close to the sense of what she held.

In these days she was keenly dramatizing herself.
She glanced stealthily sidewise at the mirror and the
Madonna look came into her face. When Bobby and
May were beside her, she drew them within her thin
little arms and pressed them to her breast with an air
of ecstasy and reverence.

But she did not care to have them close to her for

long, and if they fell into some childish dispute she called, in a peevish complaining voice, for Mamma Farley, and said that no one considered her or remembered that she was sick.

When Laurence reached home after his walk it was eleven o'clock. He passed through the still house and up the stairs to the bedroom, wondering if Winnie were asleep. When he opened the door he saw the light shining on her where she lay on the lounge with her eyes shut.

Her mop of reddish hair was tangled about her face, turned to one side on the pillows. The gold edges of her lashes rested delicately on her shadowed cheek. She heard Laurence, and stirred.

With a nauseous sense of inevitability, he waited for her to turn upon him her look of conscious sweetness.

"You were gone so long, Laurie!" She blinked at him and smiled drowsily.

"Yes," he said. "I went for a long walk."

She made a little mouth. "I've been back such a little while, I don't think you ought to leave me when it's Sunday, Laurie."

"You'll like me better if you don't see too much of me." His joke was stiff. He looked as though his false smile hurt him.

Winnie gazed at him. Her mouth began to quiver. "I get so lonesome, Laurie. Mamma Farley goes off with Bobby and May, and Alice is always poked away in her room!"

He did not answer this. "It's cold in here. Mother shouldn't have let the fire die down." He walked over to the grate and with his fingers laid some lumps out of the scuttle upon the hot coals. "Keep that shawl around you, Winnie. Hadn't I better call Mother and tell her to help you to get to bed?"

He came back to her. She did not speak to him. Tears rolled from her open eyes and left wet smears along her lifted face.

"All worn out, eh?" He touched her hair uncomfortably. "I'll call Mother. She always knows what to do for you. I don't."

She clung to his hand. "You don't hate me because I'm like this, do you, Laurie?"

"Don't be foolish, Winnie, child. You're worn out or you wouldn't talk this way." He put her gently from him. "I'm going to call Mother."

She began to sob. "You want to go! I don't want you to touch me if you hate me!"

Smiling wearily, he looked at her. It was a kind of relief to him to be unable to defend himself. "Since I make you cry, I think I'd better go, Winnie."

"Oh," she sobbed, "you make me cry by not wanting me! You hurt me so. You're so cruel!"

Still he stood helpless, not touching her. "For your own sake, you must stop, Winnie."

"If—if you call Mamma Farley in here now I'll— I'll kill myself!"

"No, you won't, Winnie." His voice shook. "But if you don't want me to call her, I won't."

Winnie became a little calmer. Then she said, more soberly, "You neglect and despise me."

"I don't, Winnie."

"You do!" She sat up quickly. Her eyes insisted on his reply.

"Do you believe that? Does my life really indicate that to you?"

Her little face was hard. "You do things for me," she contended, "but it's not because you love me!"

His smile faltered. He shrugged wearily. "It would be hopeless for me to attempt to justify myself, Winnie, but for the sake of your health and your baby" (he looked at her straightforwardly) "we must try to overcome this continual bickering."

She looked steadily with her dissolving gaze against his unpenetrated eyes. "Oh, I wish my children didn't belong to you!" she said suddenly.

He glanced away from her. "If I thought you and the children could do without me I might agree to resign my parental rights," he said with a slight sneer.

She pressed her hands together, regarding him in silence. Finally she said, "Oh, I know you'd be glad to!" She was crying soundlessly.

He does not love me.

She felt sorry for herself. She felt the slightness of her body and the fragileness of her bones. She was new and real to herself in her illusion of smallness that made it easier for her to relinquish her pride.

She turned her face from him and lay back on the pillow again. Voluptuously, she was conscious of her weakness. With infinite and exquisite contempt, she loved herself.

"Laurie?" Her fingers picked the cover. She did not look at them, but she knew them, little and thin, and remembered how small they were when he held them in his clumsiness. "Won't you kiss me, Laurie?"

Hating himself for his helplessness, he leaned over her and kissed her.

She lifted her arms to him. "Oh, Laurie, when I'm sick and you feel this way—— If I should die, I couldn't bear it!" she said.

"But you won't die, Winnie. You won't die!" He gave up, leaning his face against her hair. Why could they never touch?

He felt the child stir in her against him, and the child seemed so terrible and real that he longed for some terrible realness in them with which to understand the child.

Winnie felt the child stirring between them, and was ashamed. It kept her from remembering sweetly the slightness of her body and the smallness of her pretty outstretched arms. She was ugly and inert at the mercy of the child.

"Love me, Laurie!" she moaned. "I can't help being like this!" She was unfair to him, but the agony in her voice was sweet to her self-contempt.

"Stop, Winnie. You have no right to say things like that." He could not speak any more. He held her close up against him.

To herself she was small and ugly with child in a small dark room. She kissed his hair, stiff and bitter against her mouth. She envied him the wonder of the fear he felt for her.

But, while there was resentment in her, it elated her to inspire this horror of pity. Small and weak as she was, her hands were the hands of joy and agony. She was jealous of her closeness to death, half afraid that the doctor was wrong. She wanted to be in danger. Secretly, her weakness fed on its new strength.

"Dear Laurie," she said tenderly.

He kissed her again. "I've worried until I'm not fit to be with you, Winnie," he said. Then he got up. "I'll call Mother. You must go to sleep." With tears in his eyes, he smiled at her.

"Good night, Laurie, dear." Her voice was stifled in tears, but she smiled too.

When he went out and she was alone in the room, the recollection of his pained face made her feel that he had taken something from her that belonged to her, that she was incapable of holding.

*   *   *

After Christmas Winnie was moved into the back room over the kitchen, because it was warmer for her so.

There were a rag carpet here, an old-fashioned cherry bedstead, and a chest of drawers. On the flowered wall beside the bed hung a German print which represented a gamekeeper who had caught some children stealing apples. It was a very old print with a cracked glass. The children in the picture had strange oldish faces. The girls wore long skirts and the boy had half-length pants. The gamekeeper, with side-whiskers and red raddled cheeks, was dressed in a high hat, a short brown waistcoat, and tight trousers. To the right of him, in the foreground of the scene, two little dachshunds stood sedately at attention.

Winnie stared at the picture until she hated it.

Sharp specks of light flecked the worn green shades that darkened the windows. The room faced east and at four o'clock Winnie watched the sun set over the dim purple housetops. Then it was a flat white metal disk with a harsh rim of whiter fire. But half an hour later it was only a pinkish welter around which floated wispy clouds that looked burning hot, like feathers dipped in molten ore. By five o'clock everything had disintegrated in the lilac dust of twilight.

The doctor advised Winnie that, in order to avoid a premature confinement, she must move about as little as possible. But she was so bored when she was alone that she sometimes put on a fancy house gown, powdered her nose, and went downstairs. Every one, by an exaggerated consideration, seemed determined to make her aware of her state. As she walked she was obliged to sway grotesquely backward to balance the weight she carried before her. When she passed the long mirror in the little-used parlor, and saw herself hideous and inflated, she burst into tears.

Her mother was often at the house, and there was nothing so sickening to Winnie as the sweet platitudes which Mrs. Price was constantly uttering.

"The dear little baby!" Mrs. Price would say. "What a wonderful thing it is to be a mother!" Her flat face was alight with the sickish reflection of a memory that was growing dim.

Mrs. Farley, with no more animation, was less refined, and Winnie could say things to the mother-in-law which the mother would not have listened to. For some reason it satisfied Winnie to discuss her condition with irrelevant vulgarity. She hated her family for dedicating her to this sordid thing every minute of her life. There was something false in their heightened regard of her which existed because she was sick and weak.

She had become accustomed to feeling the baby move in her. Its life had become definite and independent of her. It lay in her, complete, as though it had no right there. Yet her mother, in particular, talked as though the child were a hope and a wonder still in dream. As though they must keep their hearts fixed upon it and pray it into being.

It seemed to Winnie that her life was being taken away and given to the child.

*　　*　　*

There was almost a frenzy about Mrs. Farley's attention to work. She got up at half past five in the morning, and in the still gray dawn when the grass in the back yard was silver with rime she took out the ashes in a big bucket and emptied them into the bin in the alley. The gray dust settled on her uncovered hair, but she did not seem to know it. Stiff locks, sticky with dirt, hung about her grimed face. Her flannel waist was half out of the band of her draggled skirt. Her hands, crimson at the knuckles, and grained with the filth of labor, clutched the ash can stiffly.

Mr. Farley knew his wife's abstraction was intended as a rebuke to him, but he wanted to hide behind it. Her continually averted face bewildered him, and at the same time left him grateful.

His life had been ruined. He had sacrificed everything. And now he was offered the opportunity to escape.

Since Helen had left the city again, the project for their future which had been forced into his mind appeared to him as a dream out of which he had been allotted the impossible task of making reality.

His wife, concentrating herself upon household things, seemed to him strong and natural. She had ground under her feet. She had selected the carpet she walked on. It was hers. When he passed through a room where she was at work and she swept dust into his eyes, he did not rebel. The grit in his eyes was the truth of her right. He had no carpet and no house in which to make his dream. He knew that, even though he had bought the house, it was hers, because she wanted it. In his uncertainty he was ashamed before her because her wants were so definite and limited.

Sometimes, in his confusion, he passed judgment upon himself before he knew whom it was that he judged. In a panic, he tried to find some sure conception of himself to hold against the ebb and flow of his irresolution. Winnie's precarious health gave him the loophole he needed. Until the baby was born, he must hold in abeyance the contemplation of his own affairs. He owed it to her.

"Poor little Winnie!" he often said. "I miss her so

when she is not at meals. She should be the first
thought of all of us now. We should let our individual
problems go until we can see her through her trouble."

His wife understood that he was excusing himself
for what he had not done. In the beginning of their
disagreement, when she was frightened with the strangeness of her situation, she had waited, in a numb agony
of quiescence, for the first legal steps to be taken.
Nothing had occurred, and she still waited. But there
was furtive listening in her attitude. She listened and,
in spite of herself, was glad.

*   *   *

The gas jet was shaded so that the glow fell only
on half the bed where the footboard made darkness
like an echo on the wall. Winnie's supper, untasted,
was in a tray on a chair: tea, black with long standing,
and shriveled toast on a chipped plate.

On the chest of drawers, glasses and medicine bottles
marked themselves in separate blackness against the
blank brilliant yellow-papered wall. In front of them
was a china holder with a bent candle beside which
some one had laid the rust-pink core of an apple.

About the big looking-glass the frame of purplish
wood was rich with satin reflections, but the glass it
surrounded was gray and still and mirrored a part of
the bed and the German print as though they were
a long way off.

The fire had burned low and the room was hot and
had a close smell.

Winnie wore a thick cotton nightdress with long
sleeves. Ruffles of coarse embroidery set stiffly away
from her thin wrists. She felt herself hot and light
against the cold pillow and the cold damp linen.

The window shades were up, and she could see the
moonlight, faint outside. The moonlight grew in the
room as the fire died down. The steady burn of the
gas flame was cold, like liquid glass flowing over the
dark.

Winnie's feet grew cold. She began to shiver. The
cold crept up her legs under her nightdress. It was
like grass growing up her.

The fire in the grate sputtered and flared out again.
It grew too bright. It stung her.

The brightness flowed into her eyes until they were
like hot pools, and she could not see.

When Mrs. Farley came to take the tray away,
Winnie had a high fever, and Dr. Beach had to be
called in the same evening.

*   *   *

It was four o'clock in the afternoon. In Winnie's
bedroom the window was slightly lifted to let in the
soft spring air. The room was flooded with an apricot-
colored glow. Pink dots of sunlight moved on the
wall.

The polished chest of drawers and the cherry bedstead were a deep rich red. There were lilac shadows
on the cool sheets hollowed by Winnie's upraised knees.

The picture of the gamekeeper dissolved in pale sunshine.

Winnie was sunk in a dream when a sudden pain widened her eyes. She sat up astonished, for she knew what the pain meant. It was like a challenge. The child had come to wrestle with her.

The pain came again and she clenched her fists until the nails made little red half-moons in her soft full palms. She had closed her eyes, but when she opened them they shone with a new and fierce aliveness.

Winnie spread her toes out tensely against nothing. Each time the pain came to her she seemed to know the whole world with her hips and thighs. Then she lay back exhausted, feeling knowledge ebb away in the tingling peace of relief.

When Mrs. Farley came into the room to carry away the soiled lunch tray, Winnie was unable to speak, but the shifting determined eyes of the older woman gave one quick glance and guessed what had come about.

Mrs. Farley ran out and called Dr. Beach and Mrs. Price on the telephone. Later she remembered Laurence.

Winnie was aware of the confusion in her room. She even understood that the physician and her mother were discussing whether or not she should be moved to a hospital. But in the reality of suffering their voices and faces were unreal.

If there had been no surcease Winnie could not have borne it, but just when she felt that she could endure least, pain went out of her like a quenched light, and she sank faintly as if into a memory of herself.

It had grown dark. A shaded lamp was lit. A nurse had come from the hospital and Mrs. Price and Mrs. Farley were sent out.

The nurse was a tall woman with a plump, sallow face and small confident eyes. Her nose was fat with widened nostrils that were slightly inflamed. Her peaked cap set up very high on her untidy gray hair. When she walked her starched skirt rattled like paper. She came and stood by the bedside and was harsh and still like the shadows on the wall.

Dr. Beach was a stooped, middle-aged man with a bald head and inscrutably professional eyes. In his shirt sleeves, he sat on the edge of Winnie's bed, rattling the chain on his vest or looking at his watch and coughing occasionally. Sometimes he spoke to the nurse in an undertone.

When he laid his cold hand, covered with blond hair, on Winnie's warm flesh, she shuddered to his touch. She hated the assertive hand on her, demanding her back out of pain. The heavy hand weighed down her glory and she sank back, dimmed.

The bent candle on the chest of drawers made another black bent candle behind it. On the wall, back of the row of medicine bottles, were other bottles that seemed never to have moved since the world began. The pictures had each their separate stillness of shadow. The print of the German gamekeeper floated, drowned, on the gray becalmed glass opposite. A heavy breath bellied the shade before the window, and swung it slowly inward. Then it relaxed heavily into its place against the sill.

Outside the moonless night, as if choked with quiet, crowded up from the empty street.

When Winnie lifted her lids a little they showed only the lower rim of the pain-flecked irises. Dr. Beach examined the purplish nails on her cold hands and felt her pulse uneasily.

Suddenly Winnie clutched at the nurse's hands, and, with eyes open and unseeing, uttered shriek after shriek.

The sick woman was lost in pain as in a wilderness. Her hands and feet were strange. The bed was strange. In the vast bed, so far from one end to the other, she had lost her feet.

She knew there was blood on her. The world poured from her, molten.

The nurse put the chloroform cap over Winnie's nose. Then her head detached itself from her body and floated over the bed. Her head danced like a golden thistle on a pool of blood.

Her lightness expanded. She was vastly light. And the body in the bed in the dark pool grew still, and small, and far off. She was pale and angry with joy.

But through the mist of herself, something leaped angrily upon her and dragged her to earth. Hot claws sank into her. She sank, nerveless, in the infinite darkness.

She was in bed again. The vast bed stretched from side to side of the unseen sky, and oscillated like a ship.

Not enough chloroform. She wanted to tell them, but they were too far away. They could not have heard.

She saw the bright things in the doctor's bag. Then long claws of steel.

She wanted to scream. Her tongue and lips were wool. She knew that far away, out of the darkness which did not belong to her, something warm and moist slipped. The child emerged from the blackness in which she was still caught.

The child passed from the torture which went on without it.

*　　*　　*

"Mrs. Farley, it's over. You can rest." The nurse leaned close. Winnie felt the nurse's breath, dry and hot as a sirocco, blown on her cold ear across the dark.

What did it matter to the rocking dark that the child was born? Her wrists floated. Her heart strained and gathered itself as if for its most profound joy.

But the great joy to which she opened, slowly transfigured itself. An ugly and living shudder ran through her. The joy refused her. At the instant in which she knew it entirely, she ceased to be. Her heart stopped beating. She fell back, noiseless.

The nurse, with the child in her lap, sat by a porcelain basin cleansing the baby with a big sponge.

Dr. Beach called her and she laid the baby in the new crib while she went quickly for Mrs. Farley.

When the nurse had returned and Dr. Beach was

working, attempting to revive Winnie, Laurence came into the room.

He saw the excitement and helplessness of the doctor. Once Winnie's eyelids seemed to twitch. Then Laurence leaned forward with a curious unconscious eagerness. He asked for only one thing. He wanted to know that Winnie was dead. Stealthily and suspiciously, he watched the corpse, hating the small relaxed body that had tortured him with its suffering. He wanted to know that there was no more pain.

PART IV

MRS. FARLEY had taken the baby, with its crib, into the nursery. She was seated in a low rocker, crying by the nursery fire, when May woke up.

Roused from sleep by her grandmother's sobs, May saw Mrs. Farley, with trembling lips that seemed withered by grief, lifting her head and swaying her thin body, one knotted hand clutched to her breast as if in unendurable pain.

"What's the matter, Grandma Farley?" May asked when she could endure the mystery no longer. She was like an inquisitive little animal, expecting to be beaten, but determined to gain its end.

Mrs. Farley pretended not to have heard. She was ashamed because she did not know how to explain her suffering to the child.

"Is—is anybody sick, Grandmother? Is Mamma worse?" May asked again with piping persistence. She saw the crib and some vagueness in it curiously agitated. "What's that?" she said excitedly.

Mrs. Farley rose stiffly, her figure half black, and half shining, against the firelight. Her spectacles glinted where they were fastened on her untidy flannel waist. Her old black skirt was glossed green where the fireshine caught in its folds. The gray down on

her cheek glistened like a mist. Separate strands of
her hair were threads of metal, hot and bright on
her head.

She turned and looked at May, a small vague figure
across the room in the white bed. May's eyes, with
their dilated pupils, were quick even in the shadow.

Mrs. Farley fumbled her hands painfully along the
folds of her skirt. "Go to sleep! Go to sleep, child!"
she said in a voice harsh with fear.

Day was breaking. Around the dark edges of the
lowered shades, livid squares of light were widening
against the wall.

With a stealthy gesture, May sunk into the bedclothes again and pulled the cold sheet up to her chin,
but her eyes, alive in her pale little face over the edge
of the quilt, followed her grandmother's movements
covertly.

Mrs. Farley thought she heard a sound from the crib,
and went swiftly to it.

May, quivering with eagerness, sat up again.
"What's that, Grandmother?"

Mrs. Farley bent lower over the crib. Her voice
choked. "That's your new little brother," she said.

May, delighted by the excitement and puzzled and
interested by her grandmother's tears, threw the covers
away from her, and, clutching the rail at the side of
the bed, pulled herself to her naked knees so that she
could look. "I want to see, Grandma Farley!" she
begged. "I want to get out." She had already slipped
one bare leg over the bar and was half way to the floor.

"Get back into bed this instant, May! You'll take

cold and wake Bobby too." Mrs. Farley lifted the baby, all wrapped in blankets, and carried it to May's bedside.

Without sympathy, and with the impersonal curiosity of a child, the little girl stared at the baby's small sharp features and dull bluish, unrecognizing eyes. She was accustomed in examining picture books to see fat children with round faces, and she thought it did not resemble a baby.

"Whose is it? Is it Mamma's?" she asked. "Where did she get it? Can I touch it?" She laid a small finger on the bundle, then drew back with a shudder of alienation. "How can you bear to touch it, Grandma?"

Mrs. Farley could not speak. She began to cry again.

An involuntary half-smile of astonishment parted May's lips when she saw the small tears gather in the dirty corners of her grandmother's eyes and slip along the flaccid shriveled cheeks and finally fall in gray spots of moisture on the cream-colored flannel in which the baby was wrapped.

Mrs. Farley felt that she should tell May something about her mother, but did not know how to begin. "Go to sleep. You'll wake Bobby. I'll show you the baby in the morning."

"It's morning already," May pointed out after a minute.

Mrs. Farley, moving away with averted face, glanced at the gray luminousness which stole under the shade and blanched the wainscot. "No matter if it is," she said. "It's not morning for you. Go to sleep."

Hesitating, May clung to the bedrail; but she slipped at last into the sheet. Soon after, in spite of her resistance, she had fallen asleep again, and lay, breathing deeply and evenly, with her lips parted in dreaming interest.

*   *   *

Laurence went out of the death chamber into the hall, where the gray light of the cold spring morning came dimly from the street through the transom. A milk cart stopped outside. He could hear the clatter of tins, as it came to a halt, and the hurrying feet of the driver running down the area steps and up again. Bottles were jostled together with a dull clink. The man outside whistled. The horse's shoes chimed on the cold hard street, and the milk wagon rumbled away, the noises blurring in distance.

There were more footsteps, dull, methodic. One man called to another. There was a musical shiver of breaking glass, curses uttered in a hoarse male voice, and the flat thud of running feet.

Laurence opened the front door and looked into the street. Above the dull housetops were stone blue clouds. The arc light burning over the pavement opposite was like a ball of pale unraveling silk. On the windows of the houses with their lowered blinds, the sunless day was reflected in livid brightness.

He could not bear the light and he turned back into the house into the darkened parlor, where the leaves of plants on the stand in the corner seemed to burn with a bluish fire. He could see the begonia leaves like pink hairy flesh, and the gray fur of fern fronds.

The long pier glass in darkness was like black silver. It was as though he had never seen himself move formlessly forward on its surface. He was cold. He could not stay there.

Softly and quickly, he went out into the hall and mounted the stairs again. He put his hand on the knob of the bedroom door and fancied that it swung inward of itself.

Dr. Beach had gone, but the nurse was still in the room. She had her back turned to the door and was folding up some clothes. The gas flame had been extinguished. The window curtains were open. Objects in the room were plainly visible, throwing no anchorage of shadow about them.

Laurence went toward the bed. He set his feet down carefully as if he were afraid of being heard.

When he reached Her, he saw She had not moved. She would never move. A sob of agony and relief shook him from head to foot.

The nurse coughed discreetly. Scarcely aware of it, he heard her starched dress rustle and her shoes creak as she tiptoed out.

He knelt down by the bed. The last hour of Winnie's suffering was yet real and terrible to him.

He pulled the sheet back from Her face. She had not moved. She was dead.

Stillness revolved about him in eternal motion.

Winnie lay in the center of quickness. She was

dead. He wanted to rush out of the circle filled with Her warmth.

The stillness revolved again.

She held Her pain shut in Her. He would never know it again.

He hated to leave the room where the silence was quick. Out of the silence his pain was waiting to grasp him.

About Winnie the house revolved in wider and wider circles at the edge of which Her quickness died away.

He threw himself into the vortex of Her terrific quiet. It caught him and twisted him and bore him to its center.

He was dead. He would never live again. He became one with the endless word. She was timeless in the bed in silence.

*   *   *

When Laurence stumbled into the hall he came upon his father.

"Well, Son, I don't know what to say! My God, I don't know what to say." Mr. Farley turned away, sobbing.

Laurence was numbed to the sound of his father's words, and waited for the echo of silence to die away.

They walked downstairs and into the living-room. Alice was in the room and Mr. and Mrs. Price were both there seated near a window. It was like a holiday—Christmas or Easter—to see the family together in the early morning in the artificial illumination.

Laurence covered his face. Alice went over to him and patted his shoulder.

"You must eat some breakfast, Laurie."

The kindness in her voice hurt him. He wanted to go away. But she took his hand and he was too sick to rebel against her, so he let her lead him forward through the portières into the next room where the table was set.

May and Bobby had been dressed early and seated at table, for they were going for the day to a neighbor's house. Over her brown serge dress that was becoming too short and tight, May wore a fancy clean white apron. The bow on her hair was of her best red ribbon, but it was already half untied and dangled in a huge loop above one of her ears. Bobby, too, was in a new blue woolen blouse. He was bibless and the porridge he was eating trickled, in gluey gray-white drops of milk and half-dissolved sugar, over his chin and down his dickey.

He could not get it out of his head that this was a celebration, and several times he had asked Aunt Alice where the presents were.

May was discreet enough to attend to her food, but she ate slowly and methodically, and was in no hurry to leave. When she saw her father led in by Aunt Alice as if he were a blind man, it seemed a part of the general strangeness and excitement.

May understood that there was something wrong with her mother. Yet her information was too meager to project anything but vague images in her mind. At one moment the unexpectedness of it all elated her.

Her eyes shone. She shuddered with happiness, and
her drawers were wet. But the exaltation, produced by
the sense of mystery, was followed by depression.
Tears gathered among her lashes and rolled down her
cheeks as she realized that her father was crying too.

After the children had been sent away, the embalmer
arrived and went upstairs, and when the wreath was
hung on the door it seemed almost as if Winnie had died
again.

The house now stood out from other houses. What
the family had wanted to conceal like a shame was revealed to the world. Their grief no longer belonged
to themselves. When they went to a window and looked
out their differentness separated them infinitely from
the people in the street. They were crushed by their
consciousness of separateness.

The day was interminable.

Toward evening, in the twilight, they sat in the living-room huddled in their chairs. Relaxed by emotion,
they looked drunk. Their gestures, as they shifted their
postures limply, were the gestures of debauch. With
bleered vague eyes, they peered spiritlessly at one another out of the shadows.

The sun had gone down and there was only a chilly
whiteness in the center of the room and in front of the
windows. In the gloom, the drunken people floated in
their senseless grief like fish. They stirred languidly,
or they got up, took some aimless steps, and resumed
their places.

No one suggested a light. They were ashamed of
their exhaustion and their dry eyes. In terror of not

caring enough, they began to talk, dwelling on harrying details in order to wring from each other the stimulus which would draw a little moisture from their dry lids.

Really, they were sick with fatigue. They wanted to sleep. They made themselves tense against weariness. They did not know whether, if they made a light, brightness would rouse them from their disgraceful torpor, or merely reveal their plight.

Mr. Farley, who had been in the death chamber, came downstairs, and when he stumbled over a stool by the door of the room he lit the gas. Then the reddish glow made jack-o'-lanterns of their swollen, inflamed faces. They saw each other and found that they could cry again. The tears came peacefully now, without effort. Their strength flowed from them under their lids. Their heads floated confusedly above the bodies to which they were secured by their attenuated necks, in which they were conscious of the nausea and indigestion of weakness.

The contemplation of so much misery left Mr. Farley as weak as jelly. But in the very completeness of his mental and physical depletion he felt relief.

At the moment when he descended from the room where the dead woman lay to the strange twilight inhabited by her sodden family, he gave up. He no longer attempted to escape from his vision of himself. With a feeling of luxury, he admitted his incapacity for change. He was brazen in his inward confession of failure. His ideals were too high. They could never be realized in this life. He could not go back. He

had a sense of utter humiliation and failure, yet, at
the same time, was subtly grateful for his degradation.
The fumes of fatigue permitted a vague indulgence to
his self-contempt. He put Helen away from him forever. Death was a bitterness and a peace.

*   *   *

Alice had set out some cold meat on the table in the
dining-room, but no one thought to eat.

From somewhere in the cold a fly came and buzzed
feebly about the frayed meat on the big sheep bone
that lay disconsolately in a congealed pool of amber-
white grease in the middle of the glossy blue dish.

No one came into the dining-room. The teapot, covered, at first, with a bloom of moisture, grew heavy, and
drops of water collected at its base. The young fly
clung to the huge flayed bone of the dead beast. It
crawled on moist, quivering legs along the dry and flesh-
less parts, only to slip back uncertainly when it clutched
at the fat.

In the empty dining-room it was as if the silence had
stripped the burned flesh from the dead bone. The gas
light shone, very bright on the stupidity of the table
at which no one sat. The tablecloth was white and
lustrous from the iron. The high-backed chairs stood
vacantly about the vacant meal, the dry, highly polished tumblers, and the clean-wiped plates.

The coffin was on a table in the parlor. It had a
movable inside which was pushed up so that the shoulders and head of the corpse protruded above the box.

Stiffly, yet as if of themselves, the head and shoulders of the corpse uprose from the sides of the coffin. The smooth, strange face, like the face of a wax angel, rose up complaisantly above the sides of the box.

The German woman at the bakery, who was out of bed with a child ten days old, had come to act as wet-nurse for the other new-born child. In the nursery, opposite the death chamber, she sat pressing the infant's lips to the stiff brown nipple on her full white breast.

It caught the nipple weakly and hungrily, but it did not have the strength to keep it. The brown teat, sloppy with saliva, fell from its small strained mouth. The baby squeezed its thumbs under its wrinkled fingers. Its hands half opened and shut. Its weak eyes did not see the nipple it had lost, and it began to cry fretfully, without shedding any tears.

The stout woman had a sense of unusualness and impropriety in allowing the dead woman's baby to take her breast, but she overcame the feeling before she permitted it to become plain to herself. With firm fingers she pressed the stiff nipple between the slobbering lips. The baby scratched her delicate skin with its soft nails. Its hands clutched in the agony of its satisfaction. It pressed and grappled with her resilient breast, and left there faint red marks of delight and rage.

It was happy. It sucked with fierce unseeing content. Its sightless eyes stared angrily. Its cheeks were drawn in and relaxed unceasingly.

When the breast slipped out again, it despaired. Its furry forehead wrinkled above its wizened face. Its

opaque eyes grew sharp and merciless with baffled desire. Like a small blind beast fumbling the air, it
moved its head searchingly from side to side, sucking.

It seemed impossible for the scrawny and emaciated
child to satisfy itself. The woman took the breast
away and the infant was angry once more. Its eyes
drew up out of sight beneath its overhanging lids. Its
whole body writhed in protest. It was a healthy child,
the woman said, because on the second day it could
scream like that.

By and by it grew tired of its rage and went to sleep.
It slept with its lids apart, like a drunken thing, showing its bleared irises. And, monotonously, vigorously,
it drew the air in and out of its mouth. It seemed angry
and merciless even in its sleep.

*   *   *

On the way to the distant cemetery, Laurence rode
in the carriage with his father. Both men were under
the illusion that the carriage remained fixed while the
confused faces in the streets were hurried past them
like bright leaves and driftwood torn by some hidden
stream.

When the hearse came to a halt near the new-made
grove, Mrs. Price, in the carriage behind them, had to
be aroused from a stupor and assisted to her feet. Her
knees shook. She gazed wildly and incredulously about,
and when they were lowering the coffin into the hole, she
exclaimed, in a tone of reproach, "Winnie! My God,

Winnie!" as if she expected the dead woman to rise in
response and give some comforting assurance.

Laurence refused to see what was going on. He
kept his eyes fixed on the bright ground, and permitted
himself to realize nothing more than that, though the
March day was fresh, the sun was warm on his back.

But as the minister's last words were said, Laurence
felt the agitation of people turning away, and something in him refused to reconcile itself to the irrev-
ocable thing which had occurred.

Recognizing no one, he walked aimlessly apart among
strange graves. Those who regarded him found in him
the same fascination and repugnance which had per-
vaded the body as it lay in the coffin. In some way he
seemed to belong to it.

* * *

Among the untended graves stood an unpainted
kiosk, the dusty stair that led to it yet littered with
leaves of the autumn past. It was a meaningless thing,
empty, like the words on the tombstones—words of
which the earth had already hidden the meaning.

The wind blew very high up the long hillside in the
cold, still sun. It shook the stiff, glossy blades of dry
yellow grass, and disturbed the small, sharp shadows
that laced their roots. The bare trees rocked heavily
from the earth, and swung their polished branches together.

On one grave a faded cotton flag drooped under an
iron star. By another was a wreath of tin and wax,

white roses and orange blossoms, soiled and spotted with rust, in a wooden case with a broken glass over the top. An iron bench had sunk into the ground, and was fixed there with a leg uplifted in an attitude of resignation. Some blue glass jars were filled with dried crocus buds and the greenish ooze of the rotting stems.

Above the hard twinkling slope of grass, the sky was a cold, pure blue. Pine trees, tall and conical, were flaming satin, dark against the flat white burning disk of the sun.

In a shining tree the white sun burnt innocently, like an enormous Christmas candle. There was happiness in the strong, bitter smell of the pine trees warmed by the sun.

The light that floated thin between their branches was sprayed fine from the circle of heat, like the stiff, hot hair of an angel, burning harsh and glorious as it floated from a halo. The wind rushed up against the trees and they stirred darkly as in a shining sleep.

The branches swayed; crossed each other; and fell back.

Among the graves there were obelisks, like paralytic fingers stripped dry to the bone, pointing up. A geranium in a pot was still on a grave like a red glass flame. Among the tombs it slept, encased in brightness.

A fruit tree in premature bloom was shedding its blighted petals. Heavily the tree, weighted with white, shed its ripe silence. The petals fell, and mingled with the satin flakes of light on the trembling grass.

The still grave posts were deep in silence. The silence was asleep. It did not know itself.

Silence crept waist high. Breast high. Drowned in itself.

It was asleep.

When the sun sank, out from the copper-blue night, from the horizon, the dark trees rolled angrily. The remote stars flashed blue sparks like a paler rage. But infinitely deep, from the night of the earth, the gray-white tombstones floated up.

* * *

Laurence could not believe in death. He did not know it. But he was sick with death, because it oppressed his unbelief. He wanted to take it into himself and understand it.

Yet the same breath which desired knowledge was filled with protest. He wanted to get away from the thing which crushed him with its unknown being— crushed him in the blankness of the still sunshine and the cold wind above the damp, new grave.

When he reached home after the funeral, the children had come back. May clung about her father. Because of her fear of him, she seemed to know him better than others knew him. For her own sake he wanted her to hate him, to keep herself separate from his pity of her.

He felt his pity for others in him like a rottenness. He would have torn the sickness out of his flesh, but it was through him, decaying him. His blood was dry.

If he saw anything unworthy, he immediately discovered its weakness, and sheltered it with his contempt. He could not be clean and strong and harsh for himself. That was why he could fight for nothing that he wished; because his enemies were inside him, and in order to destroy them he had to tear and torture himself. If the sickness in him had been his own, he could have cured it; but it was the sickness of his children, of Alice, of his father and mother.

As a young man he had never been able to carry a decision into effect, since he could never clearly distinguish his own pains from the pains of those he opposed. As a boy, his pride made him suffer with a sense of misunderstood greatness. Winnie had drunk that suffering out of him. He had drained himself dry that her agony might be rich.

Winnie had drunk his want. He was empty. His heart was old.

He flung his children away. He was free. But free was the name of a thing he had lost. While Winnie lived there was a certain vividness in his fatigue. His resentment of her had held him together.

He analyzed the family and told himself that it was a monster which fed on pain. It had grown stronger while Winnie had been weak and sick. It was yet stronger now that she was dead.

When night came he thought of Winnie, who had always been afraid to be alone, left in the dark and the silence and the wet earth. About twelve it began to rain. She was more still out there because of the rain.

He saw the plump, stiff body happy in its box. The rain softened its plumpness. The dead woman was lost in the thick night, in the rain—always.

The night said nothing, but in one place, far off, where the grave was, the night became bright and horrible. He understood the night where it came from the grave in the darkness.

The dead woman stirred. The cold was bright in the whiteness of her face. Here was where the dark ended in itself.

The rain fell upon her. He could not tear her from the rain, or from his horror of her. He was locked in his horror of her as in a perpetual embrace.

She was dead. She lived in him endlessly. Never could he be delivered except into greater intimacy. Forever, he belonged to her; to her white face with shut eyes, to its passive torture, to its movelessness against rain. He felt already the day, cold like this, still like this, when she would have him utterly. Almost, it seemed that he remembered something.

*   *   *

One evening after the children had eaten, Alice said, "I'll undress the kiddikins. Is it time for the baby's bottle, Mamma?"

Mrs. Farley wanted to give the baby his bottle, but there was meat burning in the oven, so she resigned the office to Alice. "If he's still asleep, don't wake him up."

Alice went upstairs, carrying the bottle in one hand and holding Bobby's fist with the other. May came behind.

When they reached the nursery, the baby seemed so

quiet that Alice set the bottle on the mantel shelf and began to undress Bobby.

It was summery dusk in the room. Outside the window the city melted in hyacinth mist. The gold lights in the houses across the street were still like a row of crocuses. Everything else seemed to be shaken in the trembling dusk. The room quivered, unreal.

In the half dark, May watched Aunt Alice.

"Climb into bed, Bobby."

"He didn't say his prayers, Aunt Alice."

"Well, he can say his prayers tomorrow night."

May knew that she, too, would not be allowed to say her prayers. Aunt Alice was awful. Aunt Alice in the dark, like a tower. Prayers seemed an incantation against an evil which Aunt Alice desired.

"Can you undo your own dress?"

May squirmed and bent forward. Her hand reached up to the first button.

"Here! At that rate it will take you all night!" Out of the darkness again, Aunt Alice's hand, heavy and hot and sure. She clutched May's shoulder and gave it a little shake. "Wriggler!"

The clothes slipped off. May felt her nakedness piercing the dark.

Suddenly Aunt Alice caught her and faced her about, naked as she was.

"What makes you act as though I were an ogress, May?"

Aunt Alice's hands hurt. May was no longer aware that Aunt Alice existed separate from the dark. It was shadow itself that bit into the child's flesh.

"I—I don't know." May giggled. Her eyes shone with arrested tears.

"Did I ever hurt you? Suppose I had pinched you —like this! Slapped you!"

Aunt Alice's hand flew out of the dark and fastened itself, alive and stinging, on May's cheek. It was a light slap, almost in play, but May died under it. She was stupid like a mirror. She sobbed painlessly.

"What are you crying for? Cry-baby! As if I had really hurt you!"

May did not care any more; so she went on crying.

"You ought to be ashamed of yourself! You'll wake the baby up."

May cried.

"Hush, I say!" Alice held May against her breast in a fierce, unkind, smothering hug, so that the baby might not hear her cry.

She uncurled May's loose fingers and laid them against her breast in the darkness. She wanted May to be conscious of breasts burning and unfolding of themselves. She wanted May to help her to understand her breasts.

May felt Aunt Alice big and soft under her palm. She did not want her. She had no name for the feel of her beyond the consciousness of softness which she did not like.

She was naked and chilled. Her palm sunk upon the big bosom where Aunt Alice pressed it, and she shuddered away from the yielding flesh. She did not want to know why Aunt Alice was like that. Why Aunt Alice's front swelled softly thick under her fingers. Why Aunt Alice's heart beat with a steady and terrible hammer.

"Here! Get away from me and put on your night-gown, you silly little girl!"

May was glad to be freed and pulled the gown on. Her head caught in the fabric, but she struggled through until, finally, her face peeped out—only a blind blur of face in the dim room.

"Get into bed!"

Aunt Alice sounded sharp and commanding again. May felt, more than ever, she was unloved, but, remembering the feel of the big bosom, was glad.

Free!

May scampered across the cold, bare floor on her bare feet. She braced her toes in the rail of the bed and swung herself over. Then she snuggled down—quick!

Alice could not shake off the sensation she had had with the little naked girl in her arms. The child's small, thin nakedness was like a knife. Alice wanted the child's nakedness to cut her heavy flesh into feeling.

She went over to the crib. In the dark, she could feel the baby staring up, awake, making no sound. She turned to the mantel shelf for the bottle and offered it to his lips which she could barely see. His small hands touched her meaninglessly. He accepted the bottle. He was content. She could hear him sucking.

She knelt by the crib, by the baby that ignored her. She gave herself to it. She betrayed it sweetly.

Oh, baby!

She wept, enjoying her shame. She wanted to put its hands in her breast, its lips in her breast. In the dark room she wanted to tear off her clothes to give the baby her nakedness.

But the baby could not take her. It could not show her herself. In time it would give the light of pain to some one, but now it was little with small hands.

Alice could not bear the baby any more. What did she want?

She went out of the nursery and into her own room and closed the door.

What did she want?

She began to pull her clothes off. First her blouse.

Her skin prickled with chill. The darkness was thick about her. It loved her.

Horace Ridge.

Her clothes slipped off. She pulled off her shoes and stockings and the floor and the slick matting knew her feet. The darkness knew her.

Her body was white and stiff against the dark. With a sensual agony she knew how ugly she was.

Horace Ridge.

She could not bear his name—his pain.

Through the door she could hear Laurence and her father talking as they passed through the hall.

Take this body away from me. I do not know it. I can no longer bear the company of this unknown thing.

She lay down in the bed and pulled the sheets up. Spring.

If Mamma Farley calls me to dinner, she said to herself, I shall be sick.

In the dark street a boy whistled. She heard girls

laugh. Through the window a new-leafed tree over the opposite roof moved its black foliage against the bloom of the sky, milk-purple clouds streaked with rose. A hard moon, thin like a shell, lay up there glowing inside itself with a cold secret light.

Alice felt her body harsh like the moon.

He did not love me.

They make me ugly, because unmeaning.

Beauty, straight, white, tall like a temple.

You cannot be beautiful alone. . . .

I open my heart. I take the world to my heart. I am beauty.

. . . But my body is dark in the temple.

*   *   *

"Alice!"

Alice waited a moment, smothering.

I shall not answer.

"Alice!"

Alice's lips against the crack of the closed door. "Yes, Mamma."

"Did the baby drink his milk?"

"Yes."

"Dinner'll get cold."

Alice put her clothes on, feeling as though she had been sick.

Why do I go?

She went downstairs and into the dining-room, feeling lost in the glow of the orange-colored flame that sputtered above the table. There was cream tomato soup, already served, a thick purplish-pink, curdling a little in the sweated plates.

"Hello, Alice."

"Good evening, Alice." Mr. Farley was drinking his soup timidly, and without enjoyment. Surreptitiously, his blunt fingers crumbled atoms of a crust. He did not look at his wife, but his eyes searched the faces of his children warily.

"Have your beef rare, Laurence?" Mrs. Farley asked.

"Yes," Laurence said casually. His mother always served him first. He stretched his legs under the table. He sat heavily in his chair as if he had fallen there. He took big gulps of soup and tilted his dish. Then he began to wipe butter from his knife on a ragged piece of half-chewed bread. There was a kind of satisfaction of disgust in all he did. "I hear Ridge is dangerously ill, Alice." His eyes were hard with curiosity, as he glanced at her, but not unsympathetic.

"Well?" Alice gave him a combative stare. "If you're threatening to express any satisfaction about it, please keep your mouth shut."

"I was never down on Ridge personally. He has written some fool books, but I am every sorry to hear that he is sick."

"I'd better write to him and give him your sympathy."

"No need to be sarcastic, Alice," Laurence said.

Mr. Farley coughed. "In spite of the impracticability of his views, I'm sure none of us wish Ridge out of the way."

Alice frayed the edges of her slice of beef by futile
jabs with her fork, but she could not make up her mind
to eat. Suddenly these people became intolerable to
her. She rose without a word, and walked out of the
room.

They stared at her disappearing back.

"What's the matter, Alice?" Laurence called. He
got up, glancing at his mother. "Shall I go after
her?"

Mrs. Farley had so hardened, in her determination to
keep silence, that it was difficult for her to speak of
commonplace matters. "Leave her alone," she said in
a grating voice.

Laurence shrugged and sat down again.

"She probably feels that we are not sympathetic in
regard to Mr. Ridge," Mr. Farley said. He smiled
painfully and apologetically.

"No, I don't think we are," said Laurence com-
fortably.

Mrs. Farley had shut herself up again.

Alice went out through the kitchen and stood in the
back yard. It was foggy close to the earth. The street
lamps beyond the high back wall diffused their brightness in the thickness of the night so that the darkness
seemed atingle with a whitish blush.

The light from the open door behind her streamed
out and cut the darkness with a wedge-shaped blade.
Where it fell, the grass was purple-blue milk, rich and
thick with color.

Alice walked to the alley gate, and fumbled with the
cold latch until she had opened it. Fog lay in the lamp-

lit alley like a bright breath. Up and down the street
beyond, the cold roofs were heavy on the solid houses.
Their dead finality was like a threat against the vague
and living dark.

Alice felt as though she were rushing out of herself
like an unseen storm.

She wanted to lose her body in the dark.

But, at the end of the alley, people were passing.
And she could see the square, turgid as a river, where
lights of cabs and automobiles floated, trembled, disappeared, and reappeared again. She was in terror of
them. She no longer wanted to be known to herself.

She turned, and shut the gate, and ran back up the
walk to the house.

The kitchen was vacant, bare. A moth spun in zig-
zag near the quivering gas flame. On the stove, the
pots and pans, crusted with food, leaned together, half
upset. There was white oilcloth on the table, and on
the floor a scrap of threadbare red carpet. Bread was
making in a covered bowl on a shelf back of the stove.
The baby's clothes, which Mrs. Farley had been iron-
ing, hung in a corner on a line. On a chair the bread
board was laid out with a heel of bread and a large
knife.

Alice picked up the knife. She wanted to cleave her
vision of herself.

But she must cleave it surely. She was afraid.

She dropped the knife, and, at the clatter, almost ran
from the room.

She went quickly but very softly up the creaking
back stairway. Her breath was choking and guilty.

She remembered where Laurie kept his pistol, and she passed into his room and fumbled in the bureau drawer among his clothes.

When she had the pistol in her hand, suddenly, she felt sure of herself.

She did not want to do it now. Not that night.

She was ashamed of having left the dining-room, and decided to go downstairs once more.

Before she went, she carried the pistol to her room and hid it.

She felt calm. For the first time, it seemed as if her whole body was hers, as in a love embrace. She was not afraid of understanding it. She rested in relief, in intimacy with herself. Nothing separated her from herself.

* * *

Alice threw a gray woolen bathrobe about her over her nightgown, and went downstairs to get the morning paper.

Sunlight came over the transom of the street door and blue motes floated down a spreading ladder of light. The light and the whirling motes sank into the soft dingy nap of the carpet as into a vortex. There was a deep spot of radiance, putty colored, like a pool of dust, still in the gloom.

Alice opened the door and took the paper in.

As she carried it upstairs, the steps creaked under her short, broad, bare feet.

She went into her room. The folded paper was slick and cold. It rattled as she opened it.

Her eyes ran over the columns and the gray print seemed to shift and dance and come together like the broken figures in a kaleidoscope.

Horace Ridge was dead. . . . She laid the paper on the bed.

The paper seemed a strange thing. The room, the bed, the chairs, were words. What she knew had no word.

She felt exalted—almost happy.

She dressed, and put on her hat, and placed Laurie's pistol in her bag. When she shut the pistol in the bag she had a foolish feeling that she was doing something irrelevant, but her reason told her that she had to have it.

When she opened the front door a second time, she knew that Mamma Farley was up because the milk bottle had been taken in.

The street had been washed, and smelt sweet. A child trundled a baby carriage up and down the block. The carriage went through the wet and left gray, glistening tracks where the concrete had already dried. Some negro workmen in huge clumsy coats and bulging-toed shoes went by.

Alice closed the door softly behind her. She had a vague idea that she would go to the cemetery where Winnie was buried. She would take the train a short distance and walk the rest of the way.

She reached the station. It was full of stopped clocks marking the hours of appointed departures.

The stopped clocks and the stir of people in the electric-lighted shed made one feel that the world had stopped. The motionless agitation reminded one of the restless stillness of the dead.

It was very dirty. An employee in a blue denim jacket pushed a trash receiver along the platform and carelessly swept up some piles of fruit peel and cigarette stubs, and smeared over places where people had spit.

Alice walked through the gate and out to the track. Sunshine came through the roof of the shed and burned the cinders like black diamonds. The atmosphere had a palpable texture and was acrid with smoke. An engine rushed down upon her, steaming and shining. The red cars were covered with a yellow-gray film of dust that made them orange bright. The windows glittered.

Alice climbed into the long car filled with grimy, green plush seats, and sat down by a window that was smeared along the ledge with cinders. People came in. Girls, men. A woman with a crying baby. Their faces, too, looked wan and orange in the bright clear morning sunlight.

The train started. Feeling it move, Alice was terrified. It seemed to her that already something had begun which she could not control. It was as though the train were carrying her out of herself.

Fields swept by. There was a marsh where the water twinkled with a moving shudder among the still reeds. Then came an aqueduct. On a hill were red brick houses set with shimmering glass, and above the cold

roofs the raw green of fresh leaves against the cold
pure blue of the morning sky.

A station with a neat park about it.   Another station.

Alice rose and swayed forward down the aisle of the
moving train.   At the next stop she got out.

It was lonely.   The station house was a little
deserted brick building of only one room.   Alice walked
along the dusty road between the wet bright fields.   It
was going to rain.   The sky was clotted with cloud.
Through the vapors the illumined shadows of the sun's
rays were outspread, fan-shaped, like shadowy fingers
of fire.

By itself, close to the road, was a whitewashed
wooden church, and a bush with pagan-red leaves burnt
up against it in beauty and derision.   Alice felt, all at
once, that she could go no further.   She took out the
pistol.

She looked all about her.   She was suddenly ashamed.
Feeling as though she were playing a dangerous game,
she held the pistol to her breast.   She wanted the pistol
to go off but she was afraid to pull the trigger.

She tried the cold ring of metal against her temple.

She felt herself ridiculous.   Vainly she attempted
to recall Winnie in the coffin, horrible and gone forever.

She sat down limply on a grass bank by the roadside.
The gray, motionless foliage of the trees grew thick and
cumulus against the rainy sky.   In her lax hand she
held the pistol, stupid pistol which could no longer
convince her of its purpose.   It lay inertly on her palm

that rested among the long gray grasses brushed flat to the earth with their dull crystal weight of dew.

Death.

She kept repeating the bright word to herself. She was dead. She could not believe in death.

She stood up and shook her skirts and put the pistol in the bag.

She felt stupid and sick. Her boots were all over dust and burrs clung to her petticoats. She hardly saw what was around her. She had never felt such heaviness in her life.

She walked back and sat down in the dirty little waiting-room until a train should come. Already she fretted against herself. She did not believe in death. She could not hurt herself enough. She felt herself grow mean and hard and withered in her unbelief.

She went back.

PART V

LAURENCE felt cleaner and happier in his attitude toward Winnie than he had ever been able to feel when she was alive. He did not go to the cemetery very often, but he saw to it that there were flowers planted in the plot, and that the place was well cared for.

He was cold and still inside himself. His soul had been turned to iron. And he weighed carefully in the scales of justice what had been done by her and what by him. He refused to pity her or himself.

But this could not last. His justice began to live and to ache with the pain of its own decisions. Then he threw it all away. It was only when he allowed himself to despise Winnie thoroughly that he could love her. He would not be killed with remorse.

His children were his greatest pain. He was so close to Bobby that his pride in the child was only a hurt. Laurence was harsh with the child, and before strangers did nothing but find fault.

One day Bobby dropped his toy engine out of the living-room window, and when it fell in the street a bad boy ran off with it. Bobby came crying to his father, but Laurence would give no sympathy.

"If May cried like that nobody would be surprised,"

Laurence said. "Why didn't you go out and make the
boy give it back?"

"He wouldn't div it back! He wanted it!" Bobby
bored his scrubby fists into his streaming eyes. His
sobs were futile and rebellious.

"Go out and take it away from him. Next time you
let some little ragamuffin in the street run off with your
toys, don't come to me about it. May would probably
let anybody, that wanted to, run off with the dearest
thing that she possessed, but that's no excuse for you."

Bobby was so angry that for a moment he forgot to
cry. He did not understand his father's cross words,
but they were not what he wanted and he hated them.

Unmoved in her humility, May heard herself depre-
cated. She accepted contempt as the poor take dirt.
Her father's tolerant disapproval lay on her ugliness,
but she could not think how she would be without it.

And yet he never scolded her. When her grandmother was provoked with her he only said, "Leave her
alone. You can't change her." And he always petted
her. But May knew wordlessly that he was only kind
to her. She was humble.

Something inside her died faintly. It was like a
death at the end of a sickness, a relief which she dimly
felt as defeat.

Yet she was fond of her father. She was glad he
did not scold her. She would run to meet him when he
came home from work and cling delightedly with her
little claws to his strong small hands. Mostly she was
unaware of the tightening and stiffening of his wrist
and of his readiness to loose her when she let her palm

slip from his. She was even oblivious to the contrast
presented by the spontaneity of his brusque affection
for Bobby. It was only now and then, as by some un-
named sixth sense, she knew that he was not wanting
her touch. Then she would draw back, bewildered and
ashamed of herself, but neither sad nor angry, and
would find herself in her stupidity weltering in that
same pitch-bright shadow which was always on her
soul whether she forgot it or not.

However, if he was willing to forgive her, if he felt
contrite for what he had shown, and held out his hand
to her, her heart immediately lifted. She was up above
herself in the sure definite outlines of his world, and she
was glad. She clapped her hands and danced. There
was not a spark of jealousy or reproach in her too
yielding nature.

Laurence, half concealing it from himself, despised
her subconscious forgiveness. But, since he could do
nothing to improve his relation with her, he was very
generous with candy and sweets and playthings.

The baby could sit up now, propped against pillows.
It was fat and well. It had pallid skin and red blond
hair. Its heavy cheeks hung forward and between them
was sunk its droll, loose mouth, very red and wet. Its
very blue eyes conveyed neither pleasure, surprise, nor
recognition as yet, but it showed anger, and even delight, with its hands and arms and its body, that was
long with fat bowed legs. It liked best to sit in the
bath, its weak back supported by its grandmother's
hand, and strike the clear green surface of the water
with its stiff outspread palm.

Laurence never, in his heart, admitted a relation with the baby. The child disconcerted him. He was ashamed of his intimacy with it, and that it took him for granted.

When he leaned toward it, it held out its fat arms with their creased wrists, and went to him. It sat unsteadily on his knee. The blond hair on its head was furry and lustrous and grew down the flat length of its skull at the back into the thick fold of its neck. As it moved its body its head bobbled as though it were about to topple off. When Laurence touched the baby's delicate skin he found it always damp with a cold fragrant sweat, and if he pressed the flesh it mottled with color, like a bruise.

With an eager, half-directed gesture, it would reach out and clutch his watch chain. It liked to jerk and dangle the chain. Sometimes Laurence teased it and it fretted.

Laurence said that the baby was stupid.

"Of course he can't know you! He's only four months old!" Mrs. Farley defended indignantly.

Laurence sentimentalized his mother's devotion to the baby, but that did not alter his own reaction. The child made no appeal to him. He gave it back to the grandmother. He did not want it near him for long at a time.

Occasionally when he leaned over the carriage and let its fingers stray through his stiff, gray-sprinkled hair, he lost himself in the feeble touch of its hands. It knew nothing. It did not care. It was almost as if it loved him without knowing him, and somehow he

wanted to be loved like that. It relieved him of himself.

"Eh, you little beggar!" he would exclaim, flounder-
ing with the foolish word, and he would shake its clutching finger roughly.

As the baby stared at him, it made a happy sound.
Its soul, sweet and a little blank, lay on the surface of
its eyes, and there was something awesome in its stupid
naked little looks, among the grown people who had
forgotten how to be naked like that even with themselves.

Laurence flushed and his eyes dimmed with emotion.
The softness and helplessness of the baby took his male
self. He wanted to do something for it. He could not
even buy it a sweet.

"Poor little thing! Poor little thing!" he murmured
to himself. However, the definiteness of his responsibility toward it was a relief to him in the unsettled state
of his life.

* * *

It was five months after Winnie's death before Laurence began frankly to consider his freedom and what
he should do with it. It came over him suddenly and
he knew that he must have been thinking of it before
without having realized it.

It made him feel unreal and as if he did not even
belong to himself any more.

The children had his mother and Winnie's parents,
and required no sacrifice of him. He tried to stir him-

self to rebel against the children. He might go abroad
and leave them and do some of the things which had
been impossible before.

He could not do it. He did not want to enough.
His disgust with himself gave him a sort of peace. He
flowed out of himself in his despair, like a thing too
full that has been relieved. His spirit was sodden.
There was nothing he wanted. Nothing he wanted to
do.

And yet he played with the idea of departing from
his present life. He talked vaguely about himself in
a way that disturbed Mrs. Farley's secretly growing
peace of mind. She gave him side glances but she did
not dare to show openly that there was anything to
fear.

Laurence deliberately allowed his dress to become
more and more untidy. When he met a woman in a bus
or a car he was consciously impolite. Then all at once
he saw himself inwardly and knew that women were
troubling him, that he had not actually eliminated them
in his desires.

So he went one day and found a prostitute and, as
if it were to slay something in himself, let her take him
to her room.

The experience did nothing for him. He came away
feeling sore and beaten. He resented women. He was
restless. Some unadmitted thing wanted its own in his
life.

To his father and mother he began to talk more
than ever about going to Europe.

Mrs. Farley never rebuked him when he talked of

leaving her, but her mouth drew into a pucker and he could see that she cried.

He never gave her any comfort when she did this, but after he left her it was as though he had been through an illness which had taken his strength. Her tears had drained his determination. He did not care. He was dull. He wondered what was the matter with him.

*   *   *

When Laurence looked at his mother's stooped back in its dowdy cotton dress and the wispy hair clinging to the sweated nape of her yellow wrinkled neck, her verbal acceptance of his resolution to go abroad maddened him. He was not certain that he wanted to go and he required her articulate resistance to force him to it.

Instead, she persisted in speaking to others of "Laurence's departure," as though it were already a settled thing.

Mr. Farley said, "I don't know! I don't know! You know what you want, Laurence." He felt that no one but himself understood growing old. What his wife knew of old age he did not regard as knowledge. She was old without understanding it. He had stopped writing to Helen without ever having made any definite proposal to her. He felt obliged to send her checks for their boy, but if she did not acknowledge them, though it hurt him, he was glad. He tried not to think of her. His conviction of age was born of knowledge that was deep in his flesh, and so it was good. It was beyond doubt. It was his. He felt,

without being able to express it, that truth was at the
end of things. And that what he had come to now was
truth because there was nothing more. It was the end
of life. He felt that some day it would matter very
little whether Laurence went abroad or not. Alice's
restless eccentricity troubled Mr. Farley like a dream,
but he knew that her unrest would grow weak like his
own. She would know truth as he knew it.

When he left the living-room where he had been with
Laurence and Alice, Alice said, "Papa Farley walks as
though he were a hundred."

"Maybe he is."

"You're very cryptic, Laurence."

"I'm tired, Alice."

"Well, you haven't grown tired through exerting
yourself on behalf of any one else," Alice said sharply.

"Nor have you, I think."

"I've done something for *your* children."

"I wish God had provided you with a family, Alice."

Tears rose to Alice's dull, ravaged eyes. She stared
at him helplessly. "Good God!" she said at last. "And
what are you?"

Laurence sat very still and unmoved, smiling, his pipe
between his teeth, but his lip trembled in a sneer.
"Heaven forbid that I should be expected to know!" he
said.

Alice could not bear him near her. She went out,
her heavy hips swinging with a kind of reluctant determination under her dingy rough cloth skirt, her broad,
fleshy shoulders defiantly set.

Laurence noted, familiarly, wondering why it hurt

him, how her wet, brown hair was half combed, tucked
askew; and that her collar was off the band of her
blouse at the nape of her neck, showing a patch of
swarthy skin.

She rushed up the stairs and he could hear her slam
the door of her room.   He almost imagined he could
hear her shriek as he had one time at night.

*   *   *

When Laurence talked to Alice about going away,
she said, "Good God! Go anywhere! If you had had
any guts you would have gone before this."

Mrs. Farley, hearing this, was afraid of Alice's violence, yet hoarded the consciousness of the weakness to
which it confessed.   Alice's face was already debauched
with some secret passion.   Mrs. Farley grew hard and
strong against it.

"You mustn't mention Mr. Ridge in Alice's presence," she told Laurence one day.   When she said it
she looked strong and secret.

They were at table.   Alice had not come down to
dinner.   May had been permitted the occasion to eat
with her elders.   In her small, dumb face, her eyes,
turned on her grandmother, were timidly alive with interest.   May's face was like a yellow pearl, melting in
its coldness with the terrified warmth of her blue-black
eyes.

She sat squirming in her chair, smoothing her dress
down over her stomach, but, when her grandmother
frowned at her, she undid herself.

"May, do you want——" Mrs. Farley leaned toward the child.

May knew what her grandmother thought. May was in terrible fear of being sent off to the toilet before she could tell what she had to say. "Aunt Alice talks to herself!" she blurted out shrilly.

Immediately she said it, the table surrounded by grown people melted away from her, and she was in herself, half drowned, as in a lake of pitch tingling with moonlight.

When May came out of herself, she saw her grandmother making knowing grimaces at Laurence, and Grandpa Farley looking ashamed and unhappy. Then May was sorry she had told about Aunt Alice.

"How do you know Aunt Alice talks to herself?" Laurence asked.

May looked at her father intensely, like a little surprised doe. Each experience to her was unique and absolute, like a forest creature's. There was no recognition in her seeing, and because all faces were strange to her she knew them better.

"I—I—I heard her—lots of times—in her room and when—when we were out walking." Her small hand continued to smooth her stiff dress over her hollow little belly, and she felt her ring burning a cold circle around her finger—ring that was a pain and a joy to her.

Mr. Farley, ashamed for Alice, played with his fork.

Mrs. Farley said, "Alice always had a terrible temper and got her feelings hurt needlessly, but I never imagined she would develop the crazy morbidness she has shown lately."

Mr. Farley could not bear the talk about pain any longer. He got up. "I think I'd send Alice her dinner," he said to no one in particular. He added, "I have some letters to write so I won't wait until the rest of you are finished."

When Mr. Farley was out of hearing, Mrs. Farley said, pursing her lips, "You know there was insanity in your father's family, Laurence."

"Yes. You told me once. Aunt Celia." Then Laurence frowned at his mother and nodded toward May. He hated his mother's attitude toward Alice, but, because he loathed it, he always defended it. What his instinct warned him against, he always refused to give up. When his mother, hoop-shouldered, weakly resistant, looked at him with her unyielding, self-enwrapped eyes, it was because of the very shudder which it gave him, that he hardened himself to take it. He was kind to her as an apology for his contempt.

Mrs. Farley turned to May. "Fold up your napkin."

May rolled the soft cloth in her little trembling hand. She had hoped when she spoke that her father and grandmother would somehow relieve her of Aunt Alice whom she carried inside her so oppressively, but now she knew they would not.

"Go upstairs and begin to undress yourself," Mrs. Farley said.

"Yes'm." May slid to her tiptoes. Her belly ached with a kind of sickish hunger. She went out into the

hall to the foot of the stair, and laid her pale hand on
the cold, slick rail which caught dim reflections from
the bright open door of the dining-room. She would
have to go up alone, past Aunt Alice's door. The dark
did not want her because she had told. It was white
and blind against her eyes.

Quivering in every limb she toptoed up the steps.

When Laurence was alone with his mother he said,
a little sharply, "Alice is inclined to be a busybody
and to make herself generally obnoxious, Mother, but
I don't believe her condition is as bad as you seem
to imagine. You must remember that all old maids
don't go mad."

Mrs. Farley kept her eyes away. "You don't see
what I do. You heard May. Alice has had this curious obsession of trying to separate me from her
father——" Mrs. Farley could not go on. She stood
up and began to draw off the tablecloth to shake the
crumbs out.

The gas jet hissed softly above them, and the white
curtains before the open windows were like white stirring shadows against the thick night beyond.

Laurence began to talk of some indifferent subject
and Mrs. Farley dared not bring him back to the thing
of which she wished to speak.

*   *   *

One afternoon a fancy struck Laurence to abandon
work and go out to Winnie's grave.

Summer was passing and it was half cold again. The

sunshine was a pale fluid trickling across the withering grass of the cemetery. The maples were already beginning to turn and their ghostly scarlet leaves were like pale flattened flames. He stood by the grave and heard the hissing of the wind through the sunny grass, and the rattle of husks in the cornfield that ran along the cemetery wall.

The plowed fields beyond were purple plush, misted with a fire of green. Nearer, dirty brown sheep moved over the raspberry-colored stubble. Between Laurence and the sun was glowing foliage that seemed to burn with a secret.

The sight of the mound, beaten in by the autumn winds, and already somewhat sunken, made him sick.

When he went home he said to his mother, "I've some good news for you. I've given up the struggle."

Mrs. Farley did not look at him when he said this. She was startled and afraid to answer at once. They were in the kitchen, and, smiling a little, she stared before her into the sink, by which she stood.

The clear stream of water, dancing with light, hung like a thread of glass as it flowed slowly from the shiny spigot into the porcelain bowl. The back door was ajar and the bitter-sweet smell of wet, dying grass floated into the room.

"What do you mean?" she asked at last.

He had seated himself in a careless heap near the table. His eyes were bright, and, as he gazed at her with a sharp, pained look, seemed sightless. "Just that. I have decided there is no more escape from old age in Europe than at Coney Island."

Mrs. Farley was afraid of showing how relieved she was; so she asked, "Do your father and Alice know that dinner is nearly ready?"

Laurence rose and went out of the room to call them. With a shiver of wonderment, she looked over her shoulder to watch his broad back and rocking legs as he disappeared.

Now he'll get married again, she told herself.

Mrs. Farley did not know what was occurring, but she felt herself growing strong again in the house. Her husband was coming back to her. He tried to court her favor, and, without appearing conscious of it, she showed a growing toleration for him. Winnie's death, she explained to herself, had shocked them into their senses, and she was glad with a weak, malicious gladness which she would not admit. To escape the responsibility of her own emotions, she began to go to church more frequently. Having God on her side, in her humility she felt triumphantly cruel.

But as if to conceal her relief from herself, she developed an even greater passion for self-denial than she had hitherto shown. Mr. Farley felt her shabbiness as a reproach to him, and he begged her to buy clothes, but she was always able to think of some excuse for not doing so.

Tonight, when he came into the kitchen, he had a large pasteboard box under his arm. He could not persuade her to look at it.

Her hands were in the rushing sink-water. She would not turn round.

"If you have bought me a dress," she said, "I don't

want it! You know how May needs school clothes and Laurence seems to take no responsibility whatever for her appearance, and there's that leaky ceiling in the bathroom that I have been trying to get mended for a month. You might have seen to some of those things before you spent money on clothes for me. Heaven knows it matters little enough to anybody whether I am dressed up or not." And she added, "If you insist on my having clothes you should have given me the money to buy them. I could probably have gotten something more economical and at least been sure that it fit."

Mr. Farley listened to her. He had a tired, apologetic smile, almost ashamed. He felt sorry for her and for himself. He was patient.

"Now, Mother, I think Laurence and I can promise you that the bathroom ceiling will be mended in a few days, and if you would only look at the clothes you could see whether they fit or not, and if they didn't I could exchange them."

"It isn't as if I didn't appreciate the thought——" She stopped, keeping him outside her—outside her vague, ungiving eyes. "I have to be practical for the lot of you," she said.

"Well, Mother, you can be as practical as you like about the house, but I want to keep you looking nice."

She was on the verge of retorting to him, but she restrained herself.

He felt that she was about to say something which he could not answer, and that it was time for him to leave her alone. He went out.

The room was still but for the swish of the brush that was making the white sink glow with cleanliness.

In Mrs. Farley's knotted, unsteady fingers, the back of the scrubbing brush bumped on the sides of the porcelain bowl. A fly buzzed fiercely in the luminous dark against the windowpane, then was still, like a spring that had fiercely unwound.

Mrs. Farley rested an instant. The brush slid from her fingers and clattered against a dish. She wiped her eyes with her apron. She was tired, but with weak patience, victoriously ungiving, she held out against life.

THE END